THE CHAOS AGENDA

Seth Evanoff

ISBN-10: 099092131X

ISBN-13: 978-0-9909213-1-8

To my wife,

Thank you for always encouraging me,
and not allowing me to quit.

PROLOGUE

The cattle were restless. The rancher flipped the kill switch on his ATV and sat stone still. His eyes scanned the horizon. Was it wolves? He hadn't had a run in with wolves in over a year. The Fish Wildlife and Parks had assured him that there were no active packs anywhere near his 10,000 acre ranch. For some reason that didn't make him feel any better.

Light was fading fast in the eastern Montana sky and the brightest stars were already making their nightly appearance. The rancher hopped off the ATV, grabbed his Ruger Mini 14 from its cradle on the handlebars and chambered a round. He squinted into the encroaching dusk and turned in a slow circle, looking for anything that didn't move like a cow. Nothing.

The herd said otherwise. Something was off. He turned to retrieve the spotlight from the ATV when he felt it. The ground was shaking.

"Earthquake?" he questioned aloud. It made sense. He'd heard that some animals could sense when Mother Nature was going to throw a fit.

The cattle grew increasingly nervous as they stamped the ground and jolted in small circles. It was as if they knew there was no good direction to run. The shaking had also increased in frequency, ramping up until the earth was nearly vibrating.

Fending off panic, the rancher decided it was time to head out. No use getting trampled. He returned the rifle to its cradle and mounted the

ATV. Just as he was getting ready to turn the key a light appeared several miles away. A pinprick of amber flickered for barely a moment before erupting into a ball of flame. The landscape was instantly illuminated as if a giant had just struck a match to his lantern. The glowing orb lifted slowly from the ground, gained speed and carved an arc through the night sky, leaving a plume of white smoke in its wake.

The rancher knew exactly what was happening. He'd ridden by those nuclear missile silos while mending fences since he was a kid.

"God help us," he whispered.

CHAPTER 1

CHRISTOPHER TEMPLE reclined in his seat at the back of the posh charter bus. His thumbs tapped rhythmically across the face of his smart phone as he texted the cute blonde girl, Hailey Goodman, two seats ahead.

Ah, I love choir, he thought to himself as an arrogant smirk crossed his face. Girls were the reason he'd decided to join choir his senior year of high school, that and the fact that it was a credit requirement for graduation. He could have taken art class but there weren't near as many girls and they didn't get to take an end of the year trip, like this one. Chris was especially stoked for this particular outing. After weeks of arguing and begging, his father agreed to let him travel without his bodyguard. Chris didn't see what the big deal was. Nobody else at his school had a bodyguard. He would probably just draw more attention. Besides, without his dad's babysitter he had a lot more opportunity to fool around.

Chris' concert choir class was nearing the end of their two-week tour of the northwest. After departing their private high school in San Francisco, they had put on concerts throughout Oregon, worked their way up through Washington, crossed into northern Idaho then hopped the USA Canada border. They would make Calgary, Alberta late that night. After singing in the morning they would then swing down to Kalispell, Montana for one last gig before heading home.

Chris hit "send" and peeked over the top of his seat to watch her reaction. She spun her phone around to show her friend in the seat next

3

to her. They erupted in hushed giggles then set to work composing a reply. Pete, the only other guy in choir that Chris would associate with, sat next to him in the aisle seat. Enormous headphones were clamped over his ears and he bobbed his head to a private rhythm, eyes closed, mouth hanging open. Chris thought of showing him the spicy conversation he'd been working on for the past sixty miles, but opted not to. He didn't like Pete that much anyway.

What was taking her so long? He checked again. The girls were still working. Although he couldn't see them, it was dark enough to see the pale glow of the backlit screen emanating from below their headrests.

Chris scanned the interior of the bus. At the front, Mr. Feeley the choir teacher, slept on a rolled up jacket propped against his window. The rest of the students either snored in their seats or fidgeted on their phones or tablets.

He sunk back into his seat impatiently. Two things had always made him lonely and uncomfortable: wide open spaces and darkness. Unfortunately, right now he had both. His current chat session was helping to take the edge off—a little. He just wanted to get to a city. Calgary would do.

The collective light given off by electronic devices illuminated the bus well enough to turn Chris' window into a crude mirror. He admired his fresh cut brown hair, combing it to the side with his fingers. He was good looking and he knew it. Pushing six feet tall with a fit body and rugged features, he had what it took to be a male model, including the expensive clothes. He smiled and winked at himself.

The bus crested a gradual hill and a sea of lights replaced Chris' mirror. Calgary, finally. His spirits lifted as he took in the sheer size of the man-made concrete jungle.

Suddenly, an explosion of searing light flared in the sky with such intensity that Chris had to close his eyes and look away.

"Whoa!" A student behind him exclaimed.

The flash had captured the collective attention of everyone, except Mr. Feeley who must have been exhausted from the day. Students began to pile up on Chris' side of the bus to look out the window.

Chris quickly turned back. The flash had subsided but was now replaced by several illuminated rings flowing from the epicenter like ripples in a galactic pond. The first ring rolled overhead and traveled to the horizon in every direction. As the second ring approached, the million points of light that defined Calgary vanished.

Something was dreadfully wrong. Chris instinctively grabbed his phone to call his dad. No Service.

Pete sat up in his seat and peeled off his headphones.

"Hey, let me borrow your cell phone," Chris demanded.

"Sorry dude, I don't have any service," he replied groggily.

"Alright everyone, what seems to be the problem?" Mr. Feeley was awake and stood in the aisle facing them, steadying himself on the seats.

"Mr. Feeley, something like exploded-" Chris didn't get the chance to finish his sentence before the bus driver mashed the brakes sending Mr. Feeley soaring through the air backward, smashing into the windshield and falling to the floor. The driver had been so preoccupied with the strange lightshow he failed to see the stopped SUV in front of him. The bus groaned under its own weight as he tried to avoid it. It was too little to late. It plowed into the vehicle with such force it reduced it to a tangled mass of rubber and steel before casting it into the ditch like a toy.

Chris closed his eyes and braced himself against the seatback in front of him. No amount of strength could keep his body from slamming forward like he'd been grabbed and pinned by a giant unseen hand. It felt like an eternity before the bus squealed to a halt and the hand let go, allowing Chris to drop to the floor.

Confusion. Darkness. Chaos. He managed to get up on all fours. His head swirled and he felt like he was going to vomit. Something warm and sticky was dripping from his lips and his face pulsed with agony. His nose was definitely broken. He stood and stumbled into the aisle in a dream-like stupor. Pete lay on the floor in front of him, unresponsive. Cries of help mixed with moaning called out like disembodied spirits.

Chris stepped over Pete and fumbled toward the front of the bus. His foot caught something soft and he fell over it, twisting and landing on his backside. It was Hailey. She lay on her back across the aisle; eyes open, staring at Chris.

"Help me, " her words were barely audible, "please."

Chris turned from her, picked himself up and continued to the front of the bus. He needed to find Mr. Feeley and ask him how he planned to get him home.

THE NIGHT WAS a blur of fear and confusion. Students hunkered down in their seats, sobbing and longing for daybreak. There was no order, no plan and no help.

The wreckage of the SUV they'd struck lay smoldering in the ditch. The bus driver had gone out immediately after the accident to check for survivors. Fortunately, the occupants, a man and a woman both in their fifties, were unharmed. They'd stopped on the road and stepped out to observe the strange lights when the bus crashed into their car, missing them by mere feet. They ate up the majority of the night arguing with the driver over insurance and threating with lawsuits before stomping off down the road.

Chris thought that daybreak would bring comfort. Instead it only allowed the full extent of the damage to be seen. Two students were dead and the other twelve, including Chris, had varying degrees of injury. Hailey had a fractured leg and most likely a concussion. Mr. Feeley was eventually found unconscious underneath the seats. When he regained consciousness in the early morning hours and discovered he couldn't move his legs they came to the conclusion that his back was probably broken.

The only passenger that escaped injury was the bus driver, Tom. A short red-haired man with big arms and a pot belly, Tom was living proof that wearing a seatbelt was a good idea.

Chris and some of the other students that were able to walk had exited the bus and sat on the roadside, hoping for help to arrive. He watched Tom as he cursed and yanked on a piece of sheet metal that had become jammed above the front passenger tire. He'd been trying to remove the metal for over an hour and felt confident that the obstruction was the only damage serious enough to keep them from moving on.

Vehicles passed quite regularly, passenger cars and pickups pulling campers, almost all driving away from the city. Most were loaded down with people and supplies, boxes, bedding and camping gear. Despite Tom's persistent attempts at flagging one down, he only received the rejection of blaring horns. No one stopped.

Remarkably, throughout the whole ordeal Chris had managed to hold on to his phone. It suffered a cracked screen but was still usable. Although, getting a signal was a different story. When he was able to call out he got the "all circuits are busy" message. He alternated between dialing 911 and his father. Given the choice of the two, Chris would have much rather talked to the 911 operator. He'd never been close with his dad and the older Chris got the more oppressive and controlling his father became. The only things he wanted now were the perks that came from belonging to an ultra-rich family, like a company helicopter to come pick him up from this God-forsaken highway.

"You gonna just sit there and play with that phone or give me a hand?" Tom panted as he bent over with his hands on his knees.

Chris looked left and right and then at Tom, "Me?"

"Yes you. You're about the only one around here well enough to help out and you haven't stopped messing with that stupid thing all morning!"

Chris was offended. "I'm trying to call for help."

"And how's that working out for ya? Help me get this thing free so we can get to a hospital."

Red-faced, Chris reluctantly dragged himself to his feet and trudged over to Tom. He slid his phone into his pocket and gripped the metal next to the driver's hands.

"On three, " Tom counted, "One, two...three!"

They both pulled in unison and the metal broke free with a loud screech.

"Thanks." Tom said huffing.

Chris turned to go sit down and try calling again. "Whatever."

"Alright, everyone on the bus! We're leaving!" Tom announced.

The students brought themselves to their feet as quickly as they could and started loading up. Chris made sure he was one of the first.

A GULFSTREAM PRIVATE jet swooped into Bishop International Airport in Michigan, it's tires barking on the tarmac as it touched down. The plane taxied to a private hangar where an armored limousine accompanied by a black SUV full of security personnel awaited its arrival. A young dark-haired man in a suit and glasses emerged from the back of the limo and marched to the jet as it parked, reaching the door just as the engines were whirring down. Two security officers toting sub machine guns posted themselves on each side of the door as the steps were deployed.

Jonathon Temple, the tall, sharp-featured and ruthless CEO of Temple Petro emerged with his wife Madeline in tow. He didn't look happy. Jonathon always wore a suit, but judging by the elegant ball gown that his wife was wearing they'd just been whisked away from some kind of party.

The young man extended his hand. "Good evening Mr. Temple."

Jonathon stopped, looked at his hand then straight into his eyes. "Good evening?" he growled. "Dispense with the pleasantries Zimmerman. Would you care to explain to me why I wasn't notified before the launch?"

Zimmerman retracted his hand, swallowed hard and tried to maintain eye contact. "My apologies sir. The board felt it necessary to move up the timeline. The resistance to gun confiscation in the west is reaching the boiling point. The chairman apologizes-"

"Stop right there!" Jonathon Temple stepped into Zimmerman's personal space and stabbed a finger into his sternum. "The chairman can keep his apology. My son is somewhere out there Zimmerman. The future of my company, my legacy, is lost," he moved in even closer, "and you're going to find him. Do I make myself clear?"

Zimmerman cleared his throat. "Crystal, sir."

"Good, brief me on the way to the safe house. I want to know what the devil is going on. Maddy!" Jonathon motioned for his wife to follow. She obeyed, dropping her head like a scolded puppy.

ZIMMERMAN POURED a glass of single-malt Scottish whiskey from the mini bar inside the limo and handed it to his boss.

"Talk," Jonathon commanded.

"Yes." Zimmerman thought of where to begin. "As I stated earlier, the board felt it necessary to expedite the plan based on intel from our people on the ground. When operation Achilles was finalized at the last Bilderberg meeting the detonation was slated for late fall. Thus, making life harder on the population going into the winter.

"I know. I was at the meeting. Why exactly was the decision made to execute the plan today!" Jonathon was getting annoyed.

"Sorry sir. As you know Montana, Idaho, Wyoming and parts of Washington, Oregon, and Northern California have flat out refused to comply with the president's executive order on gun confiscation-"

"And since sending in federal or UN troops would turn into one long bloody war, we hatched operation Achilles. Take away the people's electricity and isolate the west from the rest of the United States. Starvation, disease, game over. Have you forgotten that I am one of the primary architects of this plan?"

"No sir."

"Then tell me something I don't know. Why today?"

"Our asset in the Wyoming governor's office contacted the board early this morning. The governors of the western states were planning a secret meeting in Helena, Montana tomorrow. The purpose of the meeting was to form a coalition of western states. From all of our projections the west had the manpower both in civilian and military troops to pull it off."

"To pull what off Zimmerman?" Jonathon asked as he stared out the window.

"Secession," he replied. "The director felt it best to nip it in the bud so to speak. Strike before they gained any steam."

Jonathon continued to stare out the window, mulling it all over. "What was the effective range of the operation?"

"Just as predicted sir. All western states have gone dark." Zimmerman allowed a smile to crease his face. "Western Canada is also down, but that was to be expected."

Jonathon inhaled deeply through his nose before exhaling slowly. He handed the empty glass back to Zimmerman. "These are exciting times. The dollar that my grandfather built this company on is nearly obsolete and every nation on earth is in economic chaos. The engineered hell that's about to ensue will wash the myth of God and liberty from the minds of the masses. When everyone is brought sufficiently to their knees we will pick them up. We will be gods, and we will usher the world into a new age of peace and world governance."

"Yes sir." Zimmerman dared not disagree.

Jonathon leaned forward, rested his elbows on his knees and brought his hands together as if he was going to pray. "Children, our children, are the key to this future." Zimmerman was hanging on his every word. "It is of utmost importance that we find my son Christopher. Contact the NSA immediately. I want to know where he is and I want a retrieval team ready to leave at a moments notice. Do you understand me?"

"Yes sir, Mr. Temple."

11

CHAPTER 2

CHRIS SAT AT the front of the bus directly behind the driver. He had decided to abandon his old seat at the back. The bodies of the two dead students were dragged there by Tom and laid in the aisle, their faces draped with spare jackets. Mr. Feeley was propped up in his seat across the aisle, sweating and moaning. He couldn't have much time. Hailey lay across the seats behind Mr. Feeley, her leg elevated on backpacks. Her face was pale with shock. Chris tried not to look at her, repulsed by her distorted leg. No one spoke. The only sounds were whimpers of pain and fear.

Why me? Why is this happening to me? Chris questioned in his mind. *If I'd only taken art class...*

The bus growled down the highway without any regard for speed limits. The road was littered with abandoned cars, no doubt commuters that had neglected to top off their gas tanks. Tom would let off the accelerator to swerve around them but Chris swore he must have forgotten where the brake pedal was.

"Finally!" Tom exclaimed.

Chris looked up to see buildings and skyscrapers protruding into the horizon. Hope began to well up inside of him.

"We're here, it's going to be okay." Chris heard Hailey's friend assuring her.

Everyone's spirits were lifted as the bus rounded a long sweeping turn that would bring them into the city. Suddenly, Tom let off the gas and decided to use his brakes. A police checkpoint blocked the road.

"Oh great. What is this?" Tom said under his breath. An RCMP officer jumped out of the cruiser parked across their lane and held up his hands, signaling them to stop. Tom opened the side door as the officer jogged over, climbing the first couple of steps upon entering the bus.

"Are there any Canadian citizens on this bus?" He shouted.

"No," Tom responded. "We're on a choir trip from California-"

"If there are no Canadian citizens on this bus, you need to turn around and proceed immediately to the Port of Rooseville."

"Wait a minute, you don't understand!" Tom was on his last nerve. "We've got injured people, we need a hospital."

"Sir, trust me, it's no better inside the city. We're trying to contain mass rioting. The hospitals are completely overrun with wounded. They couldn't help you if they wanted to."

Tom rubbed the exhaustion out of his face with his hands. "What in the world is going on?"

"You don't know?"

"No, we've been stranded since last night and none of our phones work."

The officer looked at the students then moved in closer to Tom, not wanting to alarm them, and spoke in a hushed tone. Chris leaned in closer as well. "I don't know all the details, but last night a terrorist group detonated a nuclear device over the western United States." Tom's face went blank. "Half of North America is without power."

"Is there radiation? Are we in danger?"

"It's unknown at this time. All we know is that you can't come here. You have to turn around go to the Port of Rooseville, that will get you into Montana."

Tom thanked the officer as he jumped off the bus, shutting the door behind him. He sat, as if in a trance, staring out the cracked windshield.

Chris' hope for rescue was replaced with dread. He had to get in contact with his father, there had to be a way out of this. He tried his phone again, no signal. An idea crossed his mind. Perhaps if Tom knew who Chris' father was and how much he was worth, Chris could persuade him to crash through the roadblock and take him into Calgary - for a healthy reward of course. There must be a working phone somewhere in the city, right?

"Hey, uh...Tom. That's your name right?" Chris asked in a sickly sweet voice.

Tom's trance broke. "Hmm, what?" He turned to look at Chris.

"Look, my father is a very wealthy man. Have you ever heard of Temple Petro?" Tom's eyes burned into Chris'. "That's his company. If you can get me into Calgary, maybe help me find a phone; I'm sure my father would be very appreciative."

Tom reached over and slapped Chris across the face so hard he fell back into his seat, stunned. He jumped up and grabbed him by the shirt and pulled him to his feet so fast they came off the ground.

"What is wrong with you, you little punk?" Spit from Tom's mouth landed on Chris' face. "You're trying to bribe me at the end of the world? Look around you arrogant little snot! Your friends are hurt, your teacher's probably not going to make it and all you care about is yourself!" Tom shoved him back into his seat. "You're pathetic."

The side of Chris' face burned where he'd been slapped and his broken nose throbbed and started bleeding again. Rage built in his heart and tried to manifest in tears. He quickly composed himself, dabbing his nose on his shirt cuff. This was nothing compared to the "discipline" he

14

had received from his father in the past. He knew he was no match for Tom and his only option was to be still and shut up. Chris did agree with him on one thing, he couldn't care less about anyone on that bus.

Tom returned to his seat, threw the bus in gear and pulled a giant U-turn. "We're going to Montana!" He yelled.

WALLACE MACGREGOR careened into the Fortine Food and Fuel parking lot and threw his 1985 Ford Bronco into park. Wallace, a brown haired, stocky man in his thirties, threw open his door, stretched his back and surveyed his surroundings.

He'd been in Eureka looking for supplies when the attack happened. Always thinking before reacting, he decided to lay low and camp out on an old forest service road before heading back to his home in Kalispell, some sixty miles to the south. He was glad he did. As he came through downtown Eureka that morning, evidence of widespread panic was everywhere. Cars littered the road, some still burning. The hardware store and bank looked like they'd been hit by a tornado and the grocery store was unrecognizable. Several bodies lay on the sidewalk, no doubt looters that lacked the common sense not to take what wasn't theirs in a place like Montana.

Since he had already found everything he needed the day before, Wallace opted not to take his chances trying to salvage anything in that town. Instead he weaved through Main Street and gunned it until he reached his current location, a gas station in Fortine.

He knew his wife, Jennifer, was going to be worried sick. They had protocols for situations like this; radio the group, rendezvous at the house, monitor communications. But nothing could prepare them for the real thing. He would try to make contact with the VHF radio mounted on his dash as soon as he was within range.

Wallace grabbed his camouflage sling backpack from the floor and his Remington 870 Marine Magnum shotgun from the passenger seat. Hopefully, the owner was still around and in the mood to barter.

Wallace cautiously approached the storefront. *No evidence of looting, that's a good sign*, he consoled himself. He brought the shotgun to his shoulder and slowly opened the door with his left hand, eyes up and ears open.

The bell above the door almost gave him a heart attack. His trigger finger twitched and nearly let loose a volley of double-ought buckshot.

"Help ya?" An elderly man's voice came from behind the counter. Wallace stepped forward as he corralled his heart back into his chest. A skinny man in his seventies with a tattered cowboy hat and bushy beard stood up. He had a silver .44 magnum in one hand and western novel in the other.

Wallace lowered his shotgun. "I'm not here to cause trouble. I was just wondering if you had any gas."

"Sure I got gas. Just don't have any way of getting it out of the pumps. Electricity has been out since last night. From what I hear it may never be coming back."

Wallace was afraid he was going to say that. He was hoping the old timer would have generator backup, but not many people in America thought backup power was necessary. "How about food, water or toilet paper?"

"Your welcome to look around son, but everything is pretty much gone. I stayed open all night."

16

"Thank you." Wallace turned and did a quick search up and down the aisles, looking for anything useful. There was no food, water or toiletries to be found. There was one box of steel wool scrubbers that had fallen behind a DVD rack and small bottle of bleach that had been kicked under a shelf. He scooped them up and returned to the checkout counter.

The old cowboy marked his book with the barrel of his pistol and clapped his hands together. "Alright, what do we have?"

"I'm sorry, I don't have any traditional money-"

"Ha!" the cowboy interrupted, "That stuff isn't worth the paper it's printed on. You got any cigarettes?"

"Sorry, no cigarettes either, but I do have something you may want." Wallace lifted his sling pack over his head and dug through the outside pocket, eventually producing a box of forty .22 long rifle shells.

The cowboy whistled. "You got yourself a deal son."

The men shook on it and Wallace stuffed the items into his pack. He turned to leave when he saw a charter bus pull into the parking lot, followed immediately by 1970's International Scout with no doors and a bad camouflage spray paint job. The Scout pulled along side the bus and peeled a one-eighty in the gravel. Two men wearing surplus fatigues and carrying AR-15's piled out.

"This isn't good, " Wallace sighed as he switched off the safety on the shotgun.

CHRIS COULD TELL Tom was concerned. He was checking his mirrors every thirty seconds. Getting through the border station was a breeze. There were only a few devoted agents that remained at their post and they basically waved them through when they saw the California plates. At some point when Tom was maneuvering the bus awkwardly through the tight streets of Eureka they picked up a tail. A truckload of hillbillies with rifles hanging out their windows pulled in behind them and followed at an intimidating distance.

When Chris saw the gas station sign ahead he knew they were stopping. The illuminated fuel light on the dash was visible over Tom's shoulder. He hoped the truck would pass; maybe Tom was just being paranoid. His hopes were dashed as they pulled into the Fortine Food and Fuel and the truck followed, howling to a stop alongside them.

Tom switched off the bus, took a deep breath and gathered himself, then stood to address the students. His voice shook nervously, "We need fuel or we're not going to make it home. I'm going to check if they have any. Everyone stay here, I'll be right back."

He opened the side door and stepped out into the parking lot where two camo-clad men with AR-15's intercepted him. Judging by their appearance these guys were anything but military. One of the men was pudgy and shorter than Tom, the other significantly older with glasses as thick as pop bottles.

Chris could hear the men talking to Tom but he couldn't make out what they were saying. He kept his head down and trudged toward the store, giving short unintelligible answers as he went. The men were getting agitated, walking backwards while stooping over trying to force eye contact.

Chris had a bad feeling. Tom had no chance of protecting them and he wasn't about to become a prisoner of war to some backwoods Rambo. He checked his phone. One signal bar appeared then disappeared. If only he could get higher. He turned in his seat and looked out the windows. They were completely surrounded by densely

18

forested mountains, but he needed something close. He caught sight of a knoll that gently rose from the back of the gas station. This was his only chance. He had to act quickly while the gunmen were distracted harassing Tom.

Chris crept down the steps and waited for just the right moment to make his run for it. The men had had enough of being ignored and stopped Tom just short of the door, forming a human barricade. It was now or never. He jumped off the steps and kept low as he ran alongside the bus until reaching the back. After making sure their attentions were diverted, he made a break for the forest. Once he felt he was out of sight, he edged his way around the parking lot until he made it safely behind the store. His legs pulsed with adrenaline as he clambered up the knoll. Reaching the top, he found a clearing that overlooked the parking lot and whipped out his phone. Two solid bars. He dialed his father. It rang.

"JUST TELL US how much diesel you think you got left in that bus and we'll let you through," the pudgy man lied through his teeth.

"I already told you I don't know. I'm almost out, that's why I'm here." Tom was ready to try his luck elsewhere but was too afraid to turn his back on the men.

"What about inside? Huh, what's in the bus?" Pop bottles inquired.

"Nothing, just kids. We just need to get back to California."

The two men erupted in laughter.

"You hear that Bill?" the pudgy man mocked. "We got ourselves some Californians!"

19

Tom had enough. He didn't care if they shot him in the back. As he turned to leave the laughter ceased and one of the men grabbed the back of Tom's shirt. "Where you think you're goin'?"

Tom reacted out of instinct, slamming his shoulder into the chest of the pudgy man then shoving him to ground. Taken by surprise, his friend looked at his AR-15, obviously trying to remember how the thing worked. By the time he'd chambered a round and taken off the safety Tom had reached the bus. Huffing and puffing he slammed the door shut and fired up the engine.

Tiny holes popped through the side windows of the bus followed immediately by the semi-automatic crack of gunfire. The students started screaming. Ignoring the fact there was a Bronco parked in front of him, Tom gunned the accelerator, tossing the truck aside. The bus roared out of the parking lot and down the road as the embarrassed highwaymen emptied their thirty round magazines at the moving target.

TWO RINGS. This was the closest Chris had gotten to reaching someone since the disaster happened. Three rings. *Come on*, Chris willed his father to pick up.

"Christopher?" a concerned voice answered.

"Dad? It's me!"

"Christopher where are you?"

"I'm-" Chris was interrupted by the sound of gunfire. He turned and watched in disbelief as his bus slammed through a parked truck and sped down the road.

"No!" Chris yelled after the bus. He sprinted down the knoll, hopping downed trees and dodging limbs until he burst out of the woods and into the parking lot. They were gone. He checked his phone. Signal lost. Chris shook his head in disbelief. He couldn't believe this was happening.

Panic set in as he involuntarily dropped his phone. He looked up through tear-blurred eyes only to see two angry men converging on him.

CHAPTER 3

IMMEDIATELY AFTER Jonathon Temple's call from his son was disconnected he summoned Zimmerman and put him to work on finding Chris' position. Jonathon made it clear that he wanted results within ten minutes before dismissing his head minion. Zimmerman tripped over his own feet as he rushed out of the room and hurried to a makeshift command center in the basement. Thirty minutes later he stood outside Jonathon's open office door and reluctantly knocked on the jam.

"I said ten minutes, " Jonathon said, looking up from his laptop.

"I'm sorry sir. It took the NSA a little longer than usual to pinpoint your son's location. The system is overloaded from the disaster."

"But you did find him?"

"Yes sir." Zimmerman approached his desk and laid a tablet displaying a satellite map in front of him. "Your son's cellphone last pinged a tower here." Zimmerman pointed to a red dot in a sea of green forest.

"And where is here? What am I looking at?" Jonathon was skipping annoyed and going straight to belligerent.

"Ah, sorry." Zimmerman expanded his fingers across the screen to zoom in on the dot, revealing city and road names. "He's somewhere between the towns of Eureka and Whitefish, Montana."

'That's as close as you can get? Doesn't his phone have GPS? You should be able track him, shouldn't you?"

"I'm afraid GPS tracking is a bit of a misnomer. The receiver in cell phones do just as their name implies, they receive. They then send that information via cellphone towers. There aren't many cellphone towers in this area and without the added benefit of wifi signals we're severely restricted."

Jonathon nodded like he actually understood what he was saying. "Is the retrieval team ready?"

"Yes Mr. Temple. Are you familiar with a Mr. Alan King?"

"Of course. He was admitted to the board last year. He's the CEO of one of the largest private security firms in the world."

"That's correct sir. The board would like to make amends for inadvertently separating you from your son. The director has instructed Mr. King to loan you six of his best men."

Jonathon was tempted to smile but he didn't want Zimmerman to get the idea that he was pleased with his performance. "When will they be here?"

"Now sir, they're here now," he replied proudly.

"Then send them in!" Jonathon barked.

Zimmerman hurried to the door and gestured to someone to come in. He moved out of the way as a man so big he nearly had to duck and turn sideways to fit through the door entered the office.

"This is Mr. Kendrick, the leader of your son's retrieval team," Zimmerman announced.

Kendrick, a man in his late forties with a flattop and forearms the size of most men's calves, stood at ease in front of Jonathon's desk.

Jonathon knew his type. Just because Kendrick worked for a "security" firm didn't mean he cut his teeth on patrolling shopping malls. Most men of this caliber were ex Special Forces contracted by the government to do things regular soldiers either refused or weren't allowed to do. They were also paid a lot more. For a man of Kendrick's

age to still be in the game and breathing was an indication that he knew
what he was doing.

"I would like to speak to Mr. Kendrick alone. That will be all
Zimmerman. Please close the door on your way out."

Dejected, Zimmerman backed out of the room and closed the door
softly behind him.

Jonathon leaned forward on his desk and locked eyes with
Kendrick in an attempt to establish dominance. He didn't flinch and
Jonathon soon found himself looking away from the warrior's unsettling
icy stare. He cleared his throat and stood up tall to appear more
imposing. "Do you know why you're here Mr. Kendrick?"

Kendrick didn't miss a beat. "Yes sir. Yesterday your son was
stranded in the northwest when the grid went down. You want my team
to retrieve him."

"I take it you've done this sort of thing before?"

Kendrick smirked and answered, "Yes sir, once or twice."

"Good. And you understand how important it is that my son is
returned to me safely?"

"Yes sir." Kendrick nodded.

Jonathon dared to look into his eyes again. "I want you to use any
means necessary to bring him back to me."

"Understood sir."

Jonathon reached into his jacket pocket and retrieved a small key.
He unlocked a large desk drawer, reached in and produced a plastic
weatherproof box about the size of a brick. "This should help
negotiating with the natives, " he said, sliding the box across the desk.

Kendrick popped the latches and flipped the lid to find twenty-five
one ounce gold bars glittering back at him. He snapped it closed and
tucked it under his massive arm.

"I want you to contact me the instant you find anything." Jonathon handed him a rugged satellite phone with a folding antenna.

"Will that be all sir?"

Jonathon returned to his leather chair and pulled a cigar from his humidor. "One for the road Mr. Kendrick?"

"No sir. I have work to do."

CHRIS NEVER THOUGHT it would end this way. He always imagined his death would come by his own hand. Perhaps in a fiery crash while racing his BMW with his friends or a boating accident while partying on his dad's yacht. Now he was in the midst of a rude awakening as two strange men forced him to his knees and he stared down the barrel of a rifle.

"Look at this kid Bill, he's straight out of one of those fancy music videos!" The tall man with glasses laughed revealing a smile sparsely populated with teeth. "Are you the California kid?" he jeered.

Chris was too scared to speak and he was on the verge of hyperventilation as he drew in deep spastic breaths between tears.

"You're friends left you here California, what does that say about you?" The pudgy man poked him in the shoulder with the barrel of his rifle.

"I don't know Gabe. I don't think we'll get much use out of this one. Might as well just put him out of his misery."

Millions of thoughts blew through Chris' mind in seconds, ending in the conclusion that he had done nothing of worth with his life.

The pudgy man moved his barrel from Chris' shoulder to his forehead. Chris covered his face with his hands and let out a cry of fear.

The two men smiled at each other, obviously enjoying the pain they were inflicting on the terrified teenager.

The hefty thud of a shotgun blast rang out. The two men ducked and spun around, taken by surprise from the shot fired into the air behind them. Wallace MacGregor stood twenty feet away with his twelve gauge aimed at their faces.

"Rifles on the ground! Step away from the kid!" He gestured to the right with his shotgun. The men sidestepped away from Chris but didn't drop their rifles. "I know what you're thinking," Wallace spoke in a strong steady tone, "it's two against one and chances are one of you will kill me. It's also highly probable I'll turn one of your heads into a hollowed out melon before I go. So, I guess the question is, do either one of you feel like burying your friend today?"

The men looked at each other and nodded. The short guy pointed at Wallace. "You better hope we never see you again."

"Likewise," Wallace retorted.

The men backed away with increasing speed before turning and jogging to their truck. Wallace kept his gun trained on them until they fired up the engine and tore out of the parking lot in a frenzy of dust and flying pebbles. When they were out of sight and he could no longer hear the truck, he dropped his shotgun and exhaled an adrenaline filled sigh of relief.

Chris was sure that he died and was passing into the afterlife. He kept his hands over his face, too afraid to see where his final destination may be, until he felt a hand on his shoulder.

"Hey kid, you okay?" Wallace asked with concern.

Chris looked up like he was coming out of a dream. "Yeah, I think so."

"Good." Wallace put his hand under his elbow, pulled him to his feet, and then turned his attention to what was left of his truck.

He looked at the wreckage like he was identifying the body of his best friend at the morgue. "Ah man. I can't believe this. I bought that truck my senior year of high school. Can you believe that?" he asked turning to Chris.

Chris was still in shock. "Huh?"

"Oh, I'm sorry. My name is Wallace MacGregor," he said as he stuck out his hand.

"Chris Temple." He winced as his hand collapsed under his firm grip.

"Nice to meet you Chris, but the circumstances sure suck."

Wallace left Chris standing and returned to his truck. He dug through the interior looking for anything worth salvaging. The item of greatest importance to him was the radio, which had been annihilated, lying in two halves on the floor with a crushed circuit board. That's just great.

Chris was starting to come around. It dawned on him that Wallace might be his ticket back to civilization. He did just save his life. Maybe he could get him back to California.

He approached him cautiously. "Excuse me, Wallace?"

"Yeah," he responded without looking up.

"I was wondering if you could help me get to California-"

Wallace stopped and looked up at him in disbelief. "California?"

"Yes. My father is very wealthy and he could pay you-"

"Sorry kid. There's no way I'm taking you to California. You sure you want to go there? That place is going to be a nightmare."

Chris pleaded with him. "Please. I was on a choir trip and we got stranded. My bus driver left me here. I have no way of getting home."

27

"Look kid, " Wallace spoke with genuine concern, "things weren't going real well even before the lights went out yesterday. There are a whole lot of people out there in the same situation you're in. I have a family, a whole community that I have to get back to. I have to take care of my loved ones. I just can't help you."

Chris nodded and swallowed against the lump in his throat. "Alright. I'll just go try to call my dad again."

He turned to head back up the knoll when Wallace held up his hand and said, "Stop." He froze. Wallace turned an ear toward the road.

"What are you—"

"Shhh!" Wallace held his finger to his lips as he stared into space. "They're coming back."

"I don't hear anything."

Wallace lunged at Chris and grabbed him by the back of his hoody. Before he could react he dragged him across the parking lot then pushed him across the highway, shoving him into the brush and forcing him to the ground. Wallace lay down next to him facing the road.

"What's your problem man!" Chris protested.

"Shut up."

Chris was trying to break free of Wallace's grip when he heard the humming of tires on asphalt in the distance. He stopped struggling and laid still. Within moments the truckload of troublemakers Wallace had just run off rolled up to the gas station. Chris sunk even lower to the ground.

It appeared the men had gathered some courage and decided to re-inflate their egos. The pudgy man waddled into the store, no doubt to ask the clerk which direction their quarry had run, while the tall bespectacled one searched Wallace's totaled Bronco. A few minutes later the man emerged from the store and the two met back at the truck.

Either the clerk hadn't seen which way they had run or he wasn't going to tell. Wallace was grateful regardless.

The men were too far away for Wallace to hear what they were saying, but they were obviously making plans, drawing maps in the dust with their fingers on the hood of their truck. Once they'd agreed on a plan they mounted up and headed south toward Kalispell. Great, Wallace thought, the same direction I'm going.

Once they were in the clear Wallace pushed himself up and walked further away from the road, descending into the dense forest. Chris didn't know if he should follow or stay at the gas station and wait for help.

"Hey!" he called out, "What am I supposed to do?"

"Do whatever you want," he replied without stopping.

Chris ran after him. "I need help. I don't know where to go!"

Wallace stopped, turned around and spoke through clenched teeth. "Keep your voice down." He put his hands on his hips and stared at the ground. He knew this decision was going to be a mistake but he couldn't leave the kid on his own. "I can take you as far as Kalispell. After that you're going to have to find your own way if you still want to go back to California."

"Thank you." Chris smiled with relief.

"Let's get one thing straight though," Wallace put a finger in his face. "I will make it home alive. Which means you will not endanger my well being by doing stupid things. Furthermore, you will do everything I say, when I say it. Understood?"

Chris was rebelliously crossing his fingers in his mind but agreed.

Without hesitation he turned and headed back into the woods, giving orders as he went. "We'll parallel the highway and use the trees for cover. Keep your eyes open for any form of transportation like a car, motorcycle, bike, anything. If you see any potential threat, like our friends from the gas station, hit the ground and hide."

Chris couldn't believe how quickly Wallace was moving. While he was slipping over rotten logs and enduring slap after slap of pine bows, Wallace flowed through the forest as he ducked through branches and weaved around tree trunks. Who was this guy?

"So, what are you, like special forces or something?" Chris asked.

Wallace laughed. "No. I'm a plumber."

CHAPTER 4

THE SUN WAS getting close to dropping behind the mountains, casting long shadows and bathing the forest in an orange-red hue.

To Chris it seemed like they had been hiking for days. In reality it was only hours. He had always prided himself on having an athletic looking physique but he was now realizing that it probably had more to do with genetics than actual ability.

They trudged through the forest, keeping their distance from the highway but never losing sight of it. From time to time Wallace would stop, hold up his hand and drop to one knee. Chris would do the same. It didn't matter if it was a car passing on the road, a dog barking in the distance or some other random disturbance, Wallace wouldn't move on unless he knew it was safe.

Chris had acquired a terrible headache and he could feel himself slowing with fatigue. He thought he must have fallen on his back at some point because it felt like a heavyweight boxer had just finished rabbit punching his kidneys. He had to stop.

"Wait, wait up," he gasped.

Annoyed, Wallace stopped. "What's wrong?"

Chris felt faint so he quickly bent over. His head swirled and he knew Wallace was talking to him but it sounded as if his ears were stuffed with cotton. Darkness swallowed him and he blacked out.

When he came to Wallace was kneeling over him tapping his cheek with his hand.

"There you are kid. Wake up."

Chris propped himself up on his elbows and the headache returned with a vengeance, creeping up the back of his neck and slamming his brain like a sledgehammer every time his heart beat. He fell back to the ground.

"My head is killing me," he moaned.

Wallace felt his forehead, no fever, but he did notice that unlike himself, Chris wasn't sweating at all.

"Does your back hurt," Wallace shoved his hand under his lower back, "right here?"

"Ah!" Chris winced.

"When was the last time you had water?"

His mind was still foggy but he was pretty sure he hadn't had any fluids since before the accident. "Maybe like twenty four hours," he answered, ashamedly.

"You're dehydrated. We need to get you some water. Stay here and don't move"

Wallace left Chris lying on the forest floor and carefully approached the edge of the highway. He walked the ditch first one way, then the other, kicking at garbage, searching for something. At last he bent over and retrieved a half empty two-liter soda bottle. He unscrewed the cap and emptied the contents as he ran back to Chris.

"Alright, let's go find some water," Wallace said, hefting him to his feet. He brought Chris' arm behind his head and over his shoulder, all but carrying him. Wallace mentally kicked himself, already regretting his decision to be a babysitter.

They trudged on, stopping frequently so Wallace could catch his breath. After about an hour, while he was seriously entertaining the idea of dumping Chris and continuing alone, he heard the gurgling of a creek ahead. He put all of his strength into one last push, sweating, grunting and lugging Chris fifty yards through a group of cedars before collapsing on the bank of the creek.

The bubbling water flowed down from the mountains and through a culvert underneath the highway, snaking its way through the trees and carrying on into the darkest reaches of the forest.

Chris started crawling toward the water, so overcome with thirst he didn't care what it tasted like. As long as it was wet he was going to drink it.

"No, no, no." Wallace grabbed him from behind flipped him over on to his back. "If you drink that water and get giardia you're going to poop your guts out all night. It'll just make your dehydration worse."

"What am I supposed to do?" he whined.

"Watch and be amazed."

Wallace uncapped the two-liter bottle and dipped it into the creek filling it half way. He shook it for about half a minute and dumped it out. He then reached into his pocket, pulled out a knife, and flicked it open with his thumb.

He turned and moved toward Chris.

"What are you doing?" He looked at Wallace like an ax murderer.

"Relax kid. I just need a filter."

Wallace grabbed the hem of Chris' shirt hidden beneath his hoody. It was made of a nice synthetic material. He cut a four-inch square and ripped it in two. He took one half and stretched it over the mouth of the soda bottle to keep out debris while he dunked it under the water. Once the bottle was full, Wallace reached into his sling pack and pulled out the bleach he'd bartered for at the gas station.

"Okay. Eight drops of bleach to purify one gallon of water," he calculated out loud. "Two liters is roughly one half of a gallon. So, four drops, maybe five because the water is so cold."

He opened the bleach and poured some into the cap. Using the other half of the fabric as a sponge, he soaked it up out of the cap and squeezed five drops into the soda bottle. He immediately washed his hands and fabric in the creek, screwed the cap on the water bottle and shook it vigorously.

Chris held up his hands and motioned for the water.

"Not yet. We have to wait for half an hour." Wallace informed.

Chris' arms dropped out of frustration.

"In the meantime, I'll build a shelter."

Wasting no time, Wallace found a blown over lodgepole pine close to where they crashed. Its roots were still in the ground and the top of the pine was caught between two larger trees, forming a natural ridgepole.

He set about gathering sticks and branches from the forest floor. Starting near the ground he leaned them against the ridgepole at an angle, pushing the ends into the soft ground to secure them in place. Once finished, he whipped out his pocketknife and using a small stick as a club, started chopping pine bows off of trees by hammering the blade through the branches. He gathered the bows in his arms, returned to the shelter and began hanging them over the walls.

Chris watched with curiosity as Wallace put the finishing touches on their temporary abode by stuffing the interior with a layer of Douglas fir branches and wads of bear grass.

Wallace stood back and admired his handy work. He looked back at Chris then checked his watch. It had taken him about thirty minutes.

"Alright. Time for water," Wallace said as he helped him sit up. He unscrewed the cap and handed him the bottle. "Take it slow, and don't guzzle."

Chris tipped the bottle and poured water into his mouth until Wallace forced him to stop.

"What did I just tell you? Drink slow, you hear me?"

Chris nodded. He figured he'd better listen. The last thing he wanted was for him to take the water away, but he couldn't help giving his two cents. "This tastes like pool water."

"You're welcome," Wallace replied.

While Chris was rehydrating, Wallace poked through his sling pack and removed a small zippered nylon bag. He dropped it into a clear sealable pouch and sank it into the water at the edge of the creek, carefully piling stones on top of it and around it so it couldn't float away.

Chris sipped water until it grew so dark he could hardly see the shelter. He was starting to feel better, but as night fell so did the temperature and he found himself shivering.

"Can we make a fire?" he asked.

"Not tonight. We're too close to the road. Too many weirdo's out there right now. Let's get in the shelter, that'll warm us up."

The two crawled in, feet first, and settled into their bed of grass. The shelter was just wide enough for the two of them with the roof about eighteen inches above their faces.

Wallace stowed his shotgun next to his outside leg and used his sling pack as a pillow.

Chris was surprised at how comfortable and warm he was. When he first saw how much grass Wallace was gathering he thought it was overkill. Now he was thankful.

His thoughts drifted to the events of the day. So much had happened. It felt like days ago when his bus got stranded in Canada. His memories seemed more like bad dreams. Another feeling welled up inside of him, one that had been a stranger to him most of his life. Safety.

He hadn't really felt safe since his mother died of cancer when he was six. The devastation of her loss revisited him every time he thought about her, he had made it a point not to. Now he struggled with understanding how he received a sense of security from guy he met only a few hours ago. It was as if Wallace was what a father was supposed to be.

Wallace's voice floated in the darkness next to Chris. "My wife probably thinks I'm dead. When she finds out I'm not, she's going to kill me."

Chris attempted to make small talk. "How long have you been married?"

"Seventeen years this September."

"Cool," said Chris. Small talk accomplished.

"Yeah," Wallace wasn't done, "we got married young. It was a God thing. We both just knew. You know what I mean?"

No he didn't. What was a God thing? "Sure."

It was quiet for only a moment before Wallace broke the silence again. "Tomorrow we need to find some kind of transportation. If we had a car I could be home in an hour." He took in a deep breath. "I wonder what in the world happened."

"What do you mean?" asked Chris.

"I was in a store when the event happened. I heard people saying that we'd been nuked. I think what they meant was an electromagnetic pulse."

"Yeah, I saw it. I saw it happen," Chris said excitedly. "It lit up the whole sky. The cop up in Canada said terrorists let off a nuke in the atmosphere or something."

"It just doesn't make sense."

"What?"

"If it was an EMP, it's my understanding that it would affect almost all electronics not just the power grid. Cell phones, radios, newer cars, from what I can tell they all still work. Heck, I thought airplanes would be falling out of the sky."

Chris suddenly remembered his cell phone and frantically felt for it in his pants pocket. It was still there. Should he try his dad again? He didn't feel like he was in imminent danger. He would try him in the morning. Exhaustion ambushed him and he slipped into a deep sleep.

WALLACE AWOKE to the sound of rotor blades pounding the air. He wiped the sleep from his eyes and left Chris snoring as he picked his way through the trees and stopped just short of the highway. He squinted into the morning sky. A charcoal black military helicopter with no markings approached from the west and hovered over the road. Wallace's first thought was rescue, but something stopped him from running into the open and signaling. After several seconds it dipped its nose, picked up speed and flew north, disappearing over the jagged mountaintops.

Wallace returned to camp to find Chris up and drinking the remainder of the water.

"You look better."

"I feel better," Chris responded. "What was that noise?"

"Just a helicopter," he said nonchalantly as he pulled the bag from the water that he'd placed there the night before.

"Did they see you?" Chris asked hopefully.

"No, they didn't see me. "Let's get ready to move out. Do you remember how I purified the water last night?"

"Five drops of bleach?"

"Exactly." Wallace tossed him the bottle and the makeshift sediment filter. "Now show me."

THE COWBOY was close to finishing his western when the roar of an aircraft outside interrupted him. He drew back the hammer on his revolver and got up from his rocking chair behind the counter. He watched through the store windows as a dark helicopter descended into his parking lot, the rotor blades sucking up dirt and spitting it back out. Six men dressed in dark clothing carrying camouflage backpacks and automatic rifles jumped from the large doors on the sides. Two of the men each took an end of a large olive drab case and hefted it out onto the ground. The helicopter ascended immediately after the last man was clear, creating a temporary whirlwind before thudding off into the distance.

The leader of the group, a huge man with a flattop, used hand signals to direct his men what to do. They obeyed without hesitation, forming a semicircle facing outward in front of the store while the leader marched inside.

The bell above the door gonged just as it did with every customer, but something told the old cowboy this might be his last one. He laid his hands on the counter in full view, the pistol in his right hand.

The leader approached, eyeing the revolver but showing no concern. He skipped the introduction and instead pulled a picture from his shirt pocket and flipped it down on the counter in front of him.

"Have you seen this boy?" he asked. The cowboy picked up the picture with his free hand and tilted his head back to examine it through his bifocals. "He was traveling with a group of students on a charter bus."

His mind rolled back to the day before when he witnessed a stranger rescue that kid from some locals. He watched as they escaped into the forest across the highway.

"Is he in some kind of trouble?" he asked.

"Have you seen him?" The man leaned forward on the counter and drilled holes into the cowboy with his eyes.

His presence was so intimidating that he felt if he didn't tell the truth somehow he would know. He decided to follow his gut and try to throw him off the trail.

"Yeah, I saw that kid. Yesterday. The bus driver was looking for diesel, but my pumps weren't working. They all got back on the bus and headed south toward Kalispell." He handed the picture back.

"You're sure it was him?" he asked as he stuffed the picture back into his pocket.

"Yup. That was him."

The man looked over the cowboy's shoulder and through the back screen door of the gas station. A beat up midsized truck with a set of forked whitetail antlers screwed to the hood sat parked next to a big green garbage bin. "We need a vehicle."

"Sorry," the cowboy smiled, "she's not for sale."

"That's okay." The man slammed his left hand down on the pistol while simultaneously drawing his sidearm with his right. Before the cowboy could wrestle the revolver free, the man put two rounds into his chest. "I wasn't asking."

CHAPTER 5

IT WAS MID-MORNING and the sun was chasing the chill out of the air. Wallace and Chris had already been trekking for several hours. They got a later start than Wallace would have liked, forcing Chris to purify the water several times until he got it right. Doing this wrong could jeopardize their whole attempt at making it home he told him. There was no margin for error.

Chris was getting better at negotiating the wilderness. He was tripping less and he'd learned to hold up his arms like a boxer while walking through thick brush, protecting his face.

At first, he found the forest intimidating. An ominous maze of bushes and trees where predators lurked in the darkest reaches and followed your every move. Now, he was actually starting to enjoy the woods, though he wasn't ready to admit it.

He took deep breaths in through his nose. The air was drenched with the sweet aroma of cottonwood and pine. It was calming, nature's aromatherapy.

The two were nearing a more populated area as they began crossing gravel driveways. Chris wanted to follow them, maybe see if the home at the end could offer some kind of help. Wallace said no, it was too dangerous since most people would be on high alert and probably not in the mood to entertain strangers.

40

Chris would pull out his phone from time to time to see if he had any signal, only to jam it back in his pocket angrily. Wallace just shook his head.

"You know, cell phone towers only have twenty-four hours of emergency backup. That phone is worthless," Wallace informed him.

"How do you know so much about this stuff? You said you were plumber."

"Oh, so you must be going by the old stereotype that plumbers are overweight uneducated hillbillies that don't wear belts?"

Chris laughed. "Yeah."

"Laugh all you want kid. I worked for five years and went to apprenticeship school at night to get my license. We learned stuff like how to calculate the volume of a cylinder, flow rate, " he looked back at Chris as he was taking a swig of water, "water purification..."

Chris swallowed and nodded his head. "I get it. You're not an idiot. But how do you know about all this other stuff, like camping, survivalist stuff."

"I grew up doing it. This is Montana. We hunt, fish, camp, this is normal. Well, getting stranded during an EMP attack isn't normal, but you catch my drift."

"How did you know about the cellphone towers?"

"This might be news to you, but there's a lot of people out there that knew something like this was coming, and we started preparing for it."

Wallace stopped abruptly and motioned for Chris to get down. Wallace craned his head to see through the underbrush and then turned and mouthed, "stay here."

He crept silently toward the highway, making sure to step on soft ground, avoiding anything that might make noise. Chris saw him stop behind a giant ponderosa at the edge of the forest. He sat perfectly still for five minutes before standing up and calling to Chris. "It's clear, come look at this."

Chris jumped up and joined him as he was walked to the edge of the highway. "Look at what?"

Wallace pointed down the road. Not more than a hundred yards away Chris' bus sat motionless in the southbound lane.

AFTER FINDING the keys hanging underneath the counter, Kendrick pulled the truck around to the front of the store and briefed his men.

He pulled a topographical map from his backpack. "The clerk gave a positive ID on the boy. He said the bus left yesterday, headed for Kalispell." He circled the town on the map with his finger. "We'll take the highway south to Whitefish. If we meet any resistance on the way we'll take care of it immediately. Once we're into the populated areas we'll have to dial it back. Understood?"

"Affirmative, " the team replied.

"Mount up."

WALLACE HANDED CHRIS his sling pack so he could move easier with the shotgun. "Do not let anything to happen this. Do you understand?"

"Sure."

They approached the rear of the bus cautiously, Chris following close behind Wallace like a scared child.

Chris had mixed emotions. He wanted to know what happened. Where was everyone? But, his intentions were born of curiosity more than concern. Maybe the bus had enough fuel to make it to Kalispell.

Wallace slid up the side of the bus toward the door, taking note of the bullet holes that riddled the sheet metal and windows. He peeked around the corner of the open door and into the bus. The driver's seat was empty but the keys still dangled from the ignition.

"Wait here," he told Chris.

He ascended the steps and was met immediately by the stench of death. He felt his stomach turn and he grabbed his shirt and pulled it up over it his nose. It didn't help. Immediately to his left a deceased man lay sprawled across the seats. After quickly scanning the interior he saw two more corpses lying on the floor at the back. His gag reflex prohibited him from going any further. He turned to leave when he saw manicured toes protruding into the aisle. He swore they moved.

Outside, Chris was growing impatient. He knew Wallace told him to stay put, but who died and made him king? The thought crossed his mind that he might be able to retrieve his backpack. He was sure he still had a couple of granola bars and a soda socked away. He dropped the sling pack to the ground and sneaked up the steps of the bus.

His first breath inside bypassed his lungs and went straight to his stomach, turning it sour. He saw Wallace bent over, his upper body concealed by seats, doing something. He moved forward to get a better look when he saw Mr. Feeley, bloated and pale blue, staring up at him. His stomach flipped, his throat opened and he vomited on the floor.

Wallace's strong hand pulled him up and spun him around.

"I thought I told you to stay outside!"

"I, I..." Chris had no good excuse.

"Never mind. We have a survivor." Wallace grabbed him and pushed him forward until he saw her. Hailey was still alive.

Her broken shin was swollen and bruised and she moved her head back and forth, eyes closed, whispering pleas of help.

Chris was suddenly aware. He'd never thought of what might happen to her. Actually, he'd never even thought of her as a real person. At best she was an object to fool around with, a game to play. But now, she lay in front of him, a human life on the verge of flickering out. Chris felt ashamed of himself and sorry for her.

"Do you know her?" Wallace asked.

Chris nodded, speechless.

"What's her name?"

"H-Hailey," he managed to say.

Wallace picked up her limp hand. "Hailey, can you hear me?"

Her head stopped moving and her lids lifted just enough to reveal a sliver of her blues eyes. She tried to speak but no words came out.

"We're going to get you out of here. Okay?"

She gave a weak nod.

It was a long shot, but Wallace ran to the driver's seat sat down and turned the key. The engine whined as it tried to turn over and then shuddered, coughed and died.

Wallace returned to Chris. "We need to make a splint and get her off the bus. Where's my pack?"

Chris didn't answer he only stared at Hailey as tears welled up in his eyes. Wallace stood up and shook him by the shoulders. "Where is my pack? I told you to watch my pack—"

Wallace stopped. Chris heard it too. They both turned and looked out the back window. The men from the gas station were driving straight toward them, and closing fast.

Before Wallace could come up with a plan Chris slipped from his grip and ran off the bus. Wallace pursued and caught up with him just as he crossed the ditch into the forest, tackling him to the ground. He rolled him over onto his back and dropped his shotgun so he could pin his arms at the wrist. Chris fought and wriggled like a wild animal.

"Stop!" Wallace yelled.

"They're gonna kill us! I have to get out of here!"

Wallace heard the squeal of the Scout's almost non-existent breaks as it stopped at the bus. He let go of one of Chris' arms and covered his mouth just before they cut the engine. Bending low he whispered in his ear. "If you make a sound they will hear us and we're both dead. Now, we aren't leaving that girl behind. Do you understand me?"

Chris nodded with wide eyes.

"I'm taking my hand off your mouth. If you scream, or try to run, I'll shoot you myself."

He nodded again.

Wallace slid his hand off his mouth, grabbed his shotgun and crawled to the edge of the woods. Chris lay on his back and caught his breath. After conjuring every ounce of courage he had, he crept up next to Wallace.

From their vantage point they could see the men cautiously approaching the back of the bus, rifles at the ready. How had the men gotten behind them? They must have been patrolling side roads and they passed them at some point.

"Anyone in there?" the pudgy man called out. "Mr. bus driver, you in there?" Receiving no answer, the men lowered their rifles and approached the door.

"Look at this." The tall one bent over and picked up Wallace's sling pack.

Chris looked over at Wallace. He was shaking his head.

The tall man put the pack over his shoulder and they boarded the bus.

"Whoa! Something died in here!" The pudgy one laughed.

"Good grief!" exclaimed his friend.

Wallace watched the silhouettes of the men as they walked down the aisle. Praying they would turn and leave before they found Hailey.

"Hey, check it out," the tall man pointed, "a girl."

"Hello, beautiful."

"She's moving, she's still alive."

"Yes she is. What's your name sweetheart?" the pudgy man said loudly. "What's that? I can't hear you?" The men let out a burst of cruel laughter.

"She don't have much life left in her does she Gabe?"

"No, she doesn't," the pudgy man answered.

"What are we gonna do with her?"

He thought for a moment before answering. "I know what I want to do."

"Gabe, she's just a teenager. What about your wife?"

The pudgy man got in his face. "What? Are you gonna tell her Bill? Come on, it's the end of the world! There's no law out here!"

Wallace was disgusted as he listened to the two men argue. There was no way he could let them touch that girl. He was struck by the realization that he was her only defense. The men were done arguing.

46

"If you're so opposed to the whole thing, then just wait outside." The pudgy man handed his pal his rifle and pointed to the door.

Defeated, the tall man said, "Hurry up," and turned and walked off the bus.

Wallace had to come up with a plan fast. The tall man had both weapons now. If he could take him out first, his friend wouldn't have a chance. Although he had no regard for these men, Wallace didn't want to use the shotgun. Not only would it alert the pervert on the bus, he'd never killed a man and wanted to put it off for as long as possible.

The tall man stood by the door, leaned both rifles against the bus and dropped Wallace's pack on the ground. He reached into his shirt pocket and pulled out a pack of cigarettes, shaking one into his hand. He flicked his lighter and turned his back to Wallace to shelter the flame from the wind.

Acting on impulse, Wallace scrambled to his feet and sprinted from the forest, closing the distance between him and the man in mere seconds. He jumped on the man's back and threw his arm around his neck, locking it with his other and forming a chokehold. The man lost his balance fell backward onto Wallace, who in turn fell onto his sling pack, knocking the air from his lungs. He fought through the pain and tried to breathe through his nose as the man struggled on top of him. He saw the man's fingers searching frantically for his hunting knife on his belt. Wallace flexed his forearms and biceps and pulled back, then brought up his right knee and thrust it into the man's side repeatedly. The man stopped trying to get his knife and instead resorted to trying to pry Wallace's hands free. It was too late. The man's contorted face relaxed and his body went limp. He waited a few seconds before releasing his hold, then slowly rolled the man off of him. Wallace had just silently eliminated the first threat.

Making no attempt at stealth, he stomped up the steps of the bus to find the pudgy man trying to see over his beer belly to undo his belt.

"I thought I told you to wait outside—" the man stopped mid-sentence when he looked up and saw Wallace staring at him. "You."

Wallace's soul ignited with fierce anger when he saw the piece of scum standing by the defenseless girl. "I told you that you were going to regret seeing me."

The man launched forward and attempted a wild right hook. Wallace stepped into him, chest to chest, rendering the punch ineffective, and then hooked his left arm over the short man's shoulder. He slammed his fist into his face several times before locking his hands behind the man's neck. Wallace forced the man's head down while simultaneously bringing up his knee, pounding his midsection and face. The man was flailing his arms wildly, blinded by his own blood in his eyes. Wallace's knee was starting to get sore. He grabbed the back of his shirt flung him down the aisle, slamming his face into the already broken windshield. He collapsed in a bloody pile at the top of the steps. Wallace helped him off the bus by kicking him with the heel of his boot. The sorry excuse of human tumbled down the steps and plopped unconscious onto the asphalt.

He was in a rage and he didn't want to stop. He exited the bus and held his foot over the man's swollen face, ready to stomp the life out of him.

"Wallace!"

He stopped, foot mid-air, and looked up. Chris jogged toward him holding the shotgun out in front of him like one would hold a dead skunk. Reason returned to him and put his foot down next to the man's head.

"That was crazy!" he panted.

Adrenaline was still pulsing through Wallace's body. He inspected his scraped knuckles and then closed his eyes and took a deep breath. "Yeah, crazy."

"I thought you were dead. I was ready to run but you totally did it!" Chris was giddy, like they'd just won some kind of state championship.

The adrenaline was wearing off and Wallace's body was starting shake. He knew he didn't have much time before the men woke up.

"Go check on Hailey. I'll tie these guys up," he said, cutting Chris' celebration short.

He handed Wallace the shotgun, cupped his hoody sleeve over his mouth and nose and ascended the bus steps without complaint.

Wallace picked up his backpack and dug through it, taking inventory. He pulled out a small black nylon bag and slowly unzipped it. As he did, a clear fluid ran out and dripped onto the pavement. He shook the contents into his hand, producing two broken medicine bottles and two that were still intact. They must have broken during his struggle with the tall man.

"Dang it!" he exclaimed, kicking the ground. He returned the good bottles to their bag and carefully stuffed it into his sling pack.

Chris returned to report that Hailey was still awake. Not wasting any time, Wallace gave him his next assignment; find a cardboard box.

Chris set about searching while Wallace took care of the men. He started by tying their hands behind their backs with paracord from his pack. He then unbuckled the men's belts, yanked them from their waists and fastened them around their ankles. A quick pat down relieved the men of their knives, which Wallace tossed into the tall grass of the ditch. He turned his attention to the rifles, dropping the magazines and pulling the charging handles to eject the chambered rounds. Now they could focus on Hailey.

Chris found an empty moving box in the ditch twenty yards down the road and brought it to Wallace.

"Will this work?" he asked, handing it to him.

"Perfect. Follow me."

They boarded the bus again and Wallace knelt down by Hailey. The smell wasn't any better, but both of them were able to tolerate it.

"Hand me that jacket," he said, pointing at the seat behind Chris.

He took out his knife and made slits in the hem, then started tearing long strips of fabric about two inches wide.

Chris had no clue what Wallace was doing as he watched him cut the tape on the box and flatten it. He sliced the flaps off, then, using his hands, he curled the edges of the cardboard, forming it into a U shaped channel about two feet long.

"Hailey," he grabbed her hand again, "my name is Wallace. We're going to put a splint on your leg, okay?"

He couldn't tell if she nodded or not. Either way, the splint was going on.

"I'm going to lift her leg. You slide the splint underneath. Okay?"

"Sure...I mean yes." Chris gave a sharp nod.

"Lay the strips of the cloth down first, one every four to six inches. Then set the splint on top of them."

Wallace slowly slid one hand under ankle and one under upper calf. As he began lifting Hailey started moving and whimpering. As soon as her leg was high enough Wallace gave Chris the go-ahead. He worked quickly, placing everything just as he was told, then jumped back out of the way.

Wallace tried to set her leg down as softly as he could but the ordeal had caused Hailey intense pain. She sobbed quietly.

Wallace brought the cloth strips over the splint and put a half hitch knot in them, tightening the cardboard around her leg until it held it securely then using another half hitch to lock it in place. He made sure to tie the knots on the side of the splint so they wouldn't dig into her skin.

"Now comes the fun part," Wallace said sarcastically.

"What?"

"I'm going to pick her up and carry her to our friends' truck out there. Your only job is to carry her leg and make sure it doesn't hit anything."

Chris didn't feel like he was the right person for the job, but he knew he was the only person. His father would have never entrusted him with a responsibility like this. He felt like he was needed, like he had a purpose.

"On three." Wallace bent over the seats and put one arm behind Hailey and one under her thighs. Chris slid his hands under the splint. "One, Two, Three."

Hailey let out the loudest scream they'd heard as Wallace heaved her out of the seat and the two precariously shuffled down the aisle and descended the steps, Chris holding her leg like a tray of priceless china. After nearly tripping over the unconscious men they manipulated her body over the side of the truck and set her down crosswise in the back.

Chris ran back to the bus and returned with several rolled up jackets and a travel pillow. They slipped them under her leg to keep it elevated and propped up her head to keep it off the hard metal truck bed.

As a last order of business the two searched the bus for any food or fluids, emptying backpacks and looking under seats. They turned up a bag of chocolate chip cookies, some canned peaches, a bottled water and juice box. Chris found his backpack straight away and added two granola bars. They dropped the food into Chris' pack and hopped off the bus.

Wallace stopped to grab the two rifles he'd gotten off the men when the tall one started moving and looking around.

"Hey man," he said dreamily, "you can't just leave us here."

Wallace knelt down and looked him in the eye. "I threw your knives over there." He gestured to the ditch with his head and then stood up. He reached into Chris' backpack and dropped the water bottle by the man's face, turned, and walked away.

"Please don't leave me here!" he pleaded.

They piled their supplies behind the seats, hopped in the truck and sped off toward Kalispell.

As they were driving down the highway, Wallace turned to Chris, smiled and shouted over the noise of the wind, "You did good back there kid."

Chris smiled back. "You too."

CHAPTER 6

THE CHAIRMAN of the board of directors, a man of about eighty with thin gray hair and cold, hollow eyes, wound his way through the cherry wood trimmed halls of his high-rise office. He walked with the purpose and energy of someone half his age, wearing a pinstripe suit that cost more than a Volkswagen.

This was the moment he had been waiting for, had been groomed for, his entire life. Being elected chairman some thirty years ago had come as no surprise to him. His father served as chairman and his father before him. At that time he had only hoped that he would be the one to see a centuries old plan come to fruition, to be a scribe that would rewrite the pages of history. Today was that day.

He stopped at the conference room's towering wooden doors and straightened his tie before ducking inside. A long granite table surrounded by empty chairs ran the length of the dimly lit room. He took a seat at the head of the table and pushed a button on a console built into the granite. A giant flat-screen television hanging on the opposite wall clicked to life, displaying twelve equal squares. One by one faces appeared in each square until they were all filled. Jonathon Temple occupied the bottom right corner.

This was the board of directors, twelve of the wealthiest, most influential people in the world: bankers, media moguls and oil executives. The board had gone by many names since its inception in the 1800's: the illuminati, the Bilderberg group, and skull and bones to name a few. At some point in the twentieth century the group devised it's new moniker. The members at the time felt 'board of directors' was less apt to attract conspiracy theorists, while at the same time describing exactly who they were; hidden manipulators of world events.

The chairman cleared his throat and began the meeting. "Brothers and sisters, thank you for joining me on such short notice. I promise not to keep you long, but please bear in mind these meetings will be increasing in frequency as we proceed with the various phases of this plan."

The board received his greeting with accommodating nods and responded with the usual pleasantries.

"The purpose of this meeting is to catch everyone up to speed. I'm sure we can all agree that the past few days have been a bit of a whirlwind."

Everyone nodded in agreement.

The chairman leaned back in his chair and folded his hands on his lap. "Ms. Audet, let's start with you. Are you finding success with pushing the official story through all the major media outlets?"

Elizabeth Audet, a round-faced woman with gray shoulder length hair and a string of pearls around her neck, spoke from the top row with the absolute confidence one would expect from the CEO of one of the largest media corporations in the world. "Absolutely Mr. Chairman. We've instructed the FBI and NSA to release information alleging the nuclear missile was launched from a shipping container in the Gulf of Mexico. We're dropping breadcrumbs that should lead to placing responsibility on Iranian extremists. We have our best editors and animators concocting a supposed satellite video of the launch as we speak. We've also planted erroneous leaked information that several nuclear power plants in the west will soon be on the verge of meltdown.

The risk of radiation poisoning should help discourage people from crossing into the west. "

"And how is the population responding to the story?" he asked.

She sat up in her seat a little higher and tried to appear optimistic. "Initial findings suggest the majority of people are skeptical. The population has been exhibiting a growing distrust in the media, but we believe that through constant bombardment we can sway their thinking."

"You don't need me to tell you, Ms. Audet, that in order for the operation to be successful there is no margin for error. The people must see exactly what we want them to see, no more, no less."

"Yes Mr. Chairman."

He shifted his gaze to the middle of the screen. "Speaking of borders, Mr. Hellman, would you care to update us on the progress of sealing off the west?"

Secretary of State James Hellman, was a dark haired man with a heavy jaw and beady eyes. The owner of several corporations that controlled most of the United States food supply, he received his appointment to the president's cabinet not because he was qualified, but because he informed the president that he didn't have a choice. It was that simple.

"I've instructed the president to request UN troops to station on the eastern borders of all western states. U.S. troops won't obey orders to fire on those trying to come east, foreign troops will. They should arrive on our soil just in time for the next phase," he stated.

"Excellent work Mr. Hellman."

"Excuse me Mr. Chairman," Jonathon Temple took a gamble on speaking out of turn.

The chairman took a deep breath and collected himself, resolving to let Jonathon's outburst slide this time. "Yes Mr. Temple, what is it?"

"It's my understanding that the next phase is set to begin in two weeks. I wanted to remind the board of the current operation to retrieve my son from Montana—"

"The board is aware of the situation Mr. Temple," he interrupted. "I'm sure the team that Mr. King has so graciously loaned to you is doing all they can to retrieve your son."

"Yes, I'm sure they are. But if complications arise, if the team can't locate him, perhaps we could postpone the next phase."

The board members erupted in unanimous opposition in the form of shaking heads, sighs and some even saying, "No."

Jonathon spoke even louder, "I would ask the members of the board to put themselves in my position. If your child were caught behind enemy lines how far would you go to get them back? Especially if you knew that in two weeks a radioactive dirty bomb would be unleashed in their vicinity."

The board members were at a loss for words. The chairman stepped in. "I believe I speak for the board when I say we're truly sorry that your son was caught up in all of this," he raised his eyebrows and continued, "but, as one of the architects of this plan, you had to realize that in order to achieve success we had to remain open to changes—"

"Mr. chairman—" Jonathon knew where he was going with this, and he didn't like it.

"—and," he raised his hand to quiet Jonathon, "be willing to make sacrifices."

"All that I'm asking is that you wait until my son is out of harm's way before sending the team in with the dirty bomb."

The chairman gave Jonathon a look of pity. "I'm afraid the team has already been deployed. Mr. Kendrick and his men have orders to arm the bomb in two weeks time."

The blood drained out of Jonathon's face. No wonder the board had responded so quickly to his request for help. They were sending in a team anyway. He had to respond quickly without showing weakness. "So, you're detonating the bomb in northwest Montana? I thought we agreed that the state of Washington would be the most logical choice since that's where the Columbia nuclear power plant is located."

"At first glance it was. But, after hearing of your son's dilemma I decided Montana is as good a place as any, two birds with one stone and all that. The plan will work as long as heightened radiation levels can be detected flowing out of the west, mimicking a meltdown." The chairman cracked a creepy half grin.

"And if my son isn't found in time?" Jonathon asked, emotionless.

"I'm sorry Jonathon, we do need to be moving on. There's a lot more to cover."

"Of course," Jonathon agreed.

As the chairman continued on with the meeting, Jonathon's mind looped back to Chris. How far would he be willing to go to get back his son? His trust in the board had been dealt a serious blow. It was time to consider other options.

THE LOADED DOWN truck slowed to a stop behind the marooned charter bus. Kendrick and his men unloaded and immediately executed a search of the area. He took two men to search the bus while the others swept the surrounding area and provided security.

As they made their way around the side of the bus, one of Kendrick's men pointed as he caught site of two men wriggling in the ditch, obviously restrained at their ankles and wrists. They were oblivious to the fact they had an audience.

"I found it!" one yelled to the other.

"Then cut me loose, what are you waiting for!" the other yelled back.

Kendrick and his men approached them with their weapons lowered. These men obviously weren't a threat. They were, however, entertaining.

"Looks like you gentleman could use some help." Kendrick's booming voice startled the men at first, and then they began begging for help.

Kendrick motioned to one of his men and he drew his combat knife and cut the belts off their feet. They helped them up and brought them to the bus where they were sat down on the pavement against the front tire.

"Hey man, aren't you gonna cut our hands loose?" the tall one asked.

"No," Kendrick replied, as he squatted down in front of them. He pulled the picture of Chris from his vest pocket and held it in their faces. The smaller man's face was so swollen and bloody Kendrick wasn't sure he could even see it.

"Have you seen this boy?"

Both men leaned in, the pudgy man lifting his head to see under his gruesomely enlarged eyebrow.

"Yeah, we saw him." The tall one answered.

"When?"

"About two hours ago."

58

After putting two and two together, Kendrick was pretty sure he knew the answer to his next question. He asked anyway. "Was there anyone with him?"

"What is this man? Are you a fed or something?" he asked, disgusted.

"Yes, I am." Kendrick replied.

"Then I don't have anything to say to you." He looked away.

"Then I'm not a fed," Kendrick quipped.

"Still don't have anything to say."

"Maybe I can change your mind."

One of Kendrick's men stepped forward with the box of gold bars they'd been given by Jonathon Temple. Kendrick thought about it, but waved it off. He wasn't about to waste precious metal in negotiating with these two. There were other ways he was more comfortable with.

He reached back and unsnapped the strap on his knife and drew it from the sheath on his hip. The ominous sound of steel sliding on leather captured the detained men's attention.

"I've had a long day." Kendrick eyed the edge on his massive knife as he twisted the blade in the air in front of him. "So, my patience is wearing pretty thin."

The tall man swallowed hard and stared at his interrogator in horror.

Kendrick flicked his thumb over the finely honed blade. "I'm going to ask you just one more time. If you choose not to answer me, I'm going to skin your little friend here, and you're going to watch," he said with wide, crazed eyes.

The tall man nodded his head vigorously while the short, pudgy man lowered his head and sobbed.

"Was the boy with someone?"

59

"Y-yes," he stammered.

"Who?"

"Some guy we had a run-in with a few miles back. He attacked us, beat the tar out of Gabe here and stole our truck."

"Give me a description of the truck," he demanded.

"It's a 1972 Scout, green."

"Which way did they go?" He gestured up and down the road with the point of his knife.

"South, toward Whitefish."

"Anything else I should know?"

The man thought for a moment and then answered excitedly, like a schoolboy earning extra credit. "There was a girl! She was hurt pretty bad, all broken up. They carried her off the bus and took her with them."

Kendrick nodded. "Thank you," he said as he returned his knife to its sheath, "you were very helpful once you started thinking clearly."

He stood up and turned to leave.

"Hey! Aren't you gonna cut us loose?" The tall man's voice cracked.

Kendrick stopped, looked at him and said, "Yes, I am." He then nodded to one of his men who drew his pistol, and like a programmed machine, shot each man twice in the head.

The team convened at the truck and Kendrick gave an update. "The boy is traveling with one man and a wounded girl. They headed south in a green '72 Scout about two hours ago. We'll check the hospital first." He twirled his finger in the air. "Load up!"

CHAPTER 7

WALLACE MADE UP for lost time once they hit the road. Chris couldn't see the speedometer, he didn't even know if it worked. But, judging by how blurry the trees were as they flew past, he figured they were doing at least eighty.

Hailey appeared to be sleeping or passed out, it was hard to tell. Chris felt no less shameful for the way he had treated her, and he was also developing a deep concern for her well-being. He turned frequently to check on her, shifting pillows and adjusting things to where he believed she would be more comfortable.

Only a few miles into their journey, Wallace spotted a mound lying in his lane and downshifted to reduce his speed. Maybe it was road kill. As they got closer they both recognized the form to be that of a man lying face down on the pavement. Wallace came to stop and killed the engine. He grabbed his shotgun just in case they were being set up in some sort of carjacking ploy, and watchfully approached the body. He'd seen the man before.

Chris walked up behind him. "That's Tom, my bus driver. Is he..."

Wallace rolled him over and pushed his index and middle fingers into the flesh next to Tom's throat.

"Yeah, he's dead," Wallace said solemnly. "He must have had a heart attack or something."

Chris felt tears welling up in his eyes. He didn't even particularly like Tom, but he was a familiar face. The death Chris had seen over the past few days had been eating at the walls of the false reality he had been building his whole life. It wasn't a movie, or a video game. Tom would not re-spawn when the game was over. He was forever gone.

"Help me drag him off the road," Wallace said, slapping Chris on the back.

They each took a hand and pulled him far into the ditch. Wallace straightened out the body and crossed Tom's arms over his chest.

"Would you like to say anything?" Wallace asked.

Chris shook his head no.

"Okay, I will." Wallace bowed his head. "Father, I didn't know this man. I don't know where he came from, what he believed, or if he even has a family. I do know that nothing on this earth happens without you knowing. You knew Tom better than he knew himself. And you know where he will reside for eternity. I pray that if he has loved ones, you would comfort them and protect them. May Tom's death be used to somehow glorify you and lead others to saving faith in you. In Jesus name, Amen."

Chris never bowed his head. He only stared at Wallace, hanging on his every word. He'd been to church before, but he'd never heard anyone speak to God as if they actually knew him, let alone call Him father.

"Ready?" Wallace asked.

Chris nodded and they walked back to the truck and got under way.

For miles Chris remained silent and still. He faced forward and stared through the windshield at nothing in particular. His mind was swirling with questions. Would anyone cry when he died? Would he cry if his father died? He surprised himself when he mentally answered 'no' to that one. If he could contact his father and be rescued, where would they live? They owned homes in Michigan and Florida, but would life be the same in the eastern United States? It suddenly dawned on him that he had no desire to be with his father. No connection. No yearning. A feeling of hopeless abandonment overtook him.

"What are you thinking about?" Wallace asked.

The question roused him from his daze. "Oh, nothing," he lied.

"I'm sorry about Tom. Did you know him well?"

"No, not really." Chris squirmed in his seat, noticeably uncomfortable, and posed a question to Wallace. "What do you think happens when you die?"

"That's a big one. Do you want the long version or the short version?"

"Short version."

Wallace took a moment to condense his thoughts. "Well, I believe that everyone who's ever existed does bad things. It's in our nature, like a disease. I believe that the one who created mankind is perfect, incapable of doing bad things. That creates a problem though, because He can't really hang out with evil. Actually, His nature requires that He punish evil. Am I losing you yet?"

"No," Chris replied, intrigued.

"Good. So, God can't hang out with his creation, but He wants to because He loves us. God is smart though, and he had a plan. He became a man and took the punishment we deserve and died in our place. We're talking about God though, death was no match for him, and three days later he came back to life."

"Are you talking about Jesus?" Chris asked. He'd heard the resurrection story at an Easter service once, but no one had ever explained it this simply.

"That's Him," Wallace replied. "Now, since He's paid the price, we can hang out with Him by admitting we need His forgiveness, taking Him

63

at His word that He is who He says He is, and accepting what He's done for us. It's a gift."

Chris nodded. It was a lot to digest. "So, you never really answered my question. What do you think happens when you die?"

"The people who've had their sins forgiven go to be with Him, and the ones who choose to reject his forgiveness suffer the penalty of their sins forever."

Chris snickered. He didn't know if he was ready to believe in all this spiritual stuff. Since childhood he'd been taught that you make your own fate, essentially you are your own god. Still, something deep within was prodding him not to discount what Wallace was saying.

"Check it out." Wallace pointed to a green sign on the side of the road that read, 'Whitefish 21 miles'. "We're almost there."

KNOWING HOW CLOSE they were made twenty miles feel like an eternity. Wallace and Chris could tell they were getting close. They were seeing more houses and passing more cars. Some people even waved as they drove by.

When they finally arrived in Whitefish it felt as though they were driving out of a nightmare and into a dream. The town was picturesque. Narrow streets crisscrossed through city blocks packed with turn-of-the-century brick buildings. Main Street consisted of storefront after storefront of restored and dolled up shops, trendy clothing stores, bars, coffee shops and cafes. It was the quintessential American small town.

To the amazement of Wallace and Chris, aside from the traffic lights not working, the town seemed to be functioning almost normal.

Cars still occupied parking spaces and people still roamed sidewalks, albeit most of them were carrying some sort of firearm.

They picked their way through the old town until Main Street opened into a four lane highway. Wallace knew exactly where the hospital was; he'd worked on several plumbing projects there over the years. They broke left at the 'emergency' sign and followed a winding road through a grove of pine trees. On the other side sat a modern looking facility that didn't seem to fit in with the rest of the town. Wallace followed the road around the building and rumbled to a stop underneath the emergency room drop off.

WALLACE LEFT CHRIS to watch over Hailey while he entered the hospital to get help. He could hear the hum of machinery coming from somewhere, and to his surprise the automatic doors parted as he approached. The hospital's generators obviously hadn't run out of fuel.

The inside of the emergency room was what one would expect from a newer facility, an orderly sterile environment camouflaged with soft pastel wall paper and framed paintings of still life. A long check-in counter spanned almost the entire width of the foyer, and exam rooms opened into hallways on each end of the counter.

There was no one manning the front desk, but Wallace could hear voices coming from one of the exam rooms. He tapped his fingers nervously on the counter clearing his throat and trying to make enough noise to draw some attention.

Just as he was about to step into the hallway and track somebody down, a middle-aged female nurse with straight brown hair wearing purple scrubs appeared in the doorway of one of the exam rooms. She snapped off her exam gloves and pitched them into a garbage can by the door.

"Excuse me..." Wallace called out.

The nurse held up her finger, signaling him to wait, and stomped across the hallway disappearing through another door. Moments later she reappeared carrying supplies that she nearly threw into the exam room she had just left. She then stepped quickly behind the counter, straightened some papers, picked up a pen, looked at Wallace and asked, "Yes?"

Wallace read her nametag and it was apparent that Brenda the R.N. was more than a little stressed out. He tried to tread lightly. "I have girl who's hurt. She has a broken leg, maybe a concussion –"

"There's a wheelchair right there, " Brenda pointed with her pen, "it's going to be quite a wait, half the hospital staff didn't show up today."

Wallace was about to ask her if anyone could help them get Hailey out of the truck when she turned and vanished through another door. Shaking his head, he grabbed the wheelchair and steered it outside.

Getting Hailey out of the truck and into the wheelchair proved to be a challenge. At least when they put her in the truck she was awake and able to keep her body stiff. Now she was a one hundred pound sack of potatoes. When they finally wrestled her limp body into the chair, Wallace sent Chris inside with her while he parked the truck.

He killed the ignition and it dawned on him that since their vehicle didn't even have doors all of their supplies were vulnerable. He wasn't about to try to bring two AR-15's and a shotgun into a hospital. He contemplated his options and made a compromise with himself. He found enough room in his sling pack to cram the remainder of the food and the extra magazines. He then turned his attention to the AR-15's. Using the bullet tip from one the 5.56 rounds, he pushed out the takedown pins, separated the upper and lower receivers and removed the bolt carrier assemblies. Unless someone happened to have the right spare parts, the rifles were useless.

The shotgun was a different story. He'd saved up money from recycling copper for years to buy that gun. He grabbed the sling pack and the twelve gauge and walked quickly to the door, hiding the shotgun as best as he could by holding it against his leg. Once he got to the door he looked around to make sure no one was looking and stashed the shotgun between a row of shrubs and the building foundation. He felt like he was leaving a child alone for the first time.

IT DIDN'T TAKE LONG for Brenda to set Hailey up in an exam room. The men lifted her onto the bed and Brenda took her vitals and started her on an IV. She worked quickly and precisely, and then disappeared, as she had a habit doing.

Chris and Wallace slumped in uncomfortable hospital chairs next to the bed, fighting off fatigue as minutes bled into hours.

Wallace didn't realize that he had fallen asleep until a knock on the open exam room door jolted him awake. An older gentleman with thin, round glasses and a handlebar mustache walked into the room. If he was a doctor he sure didn't fit the bill with his boot cut blue jeans complete with a giant buckle, cowboy boots and a plaid shirt. The only thing that gave away his profession was the stethoscope hanging around his neck.

"Doctor Burke," he said, extending his hand.

"Wallace MacGregor," he responded. He shook his hand and was taken aback by the vise-like power and roughness of the doctor's grip. They'd definitely put their time in on a ranch.

"Who's the young lady?" He turned his attention to his patient.

"Her name's Hailey," Chris offered.

"Can you tell me what happened?"

"We were in a bus accident. We ran into a parked SUV, everybody flew into whatever was in front of them."

"I see," Doctor Burke said as he sat on an exam stool. He wheeled himself over to Hailey's leg and looked it over. "This is a nice splint, you guys did a good job."

He continued to give Hailey a thorough examination, checking pupil dilation, her neck and spine, and listening to her heart and lungs. "Her breathing is fine and her pulse is pretty strong. She does have a mild concussion. I'm going to get radiology down here to take an x-ray of this leg. Once we know exactly what's going on in there we'll get a cast on it." He stood and turned to Wallace and Chris. "Anything I can get for you boys? Are you hungry?"

Chris and Wallace turned to each other and collectively answered, "Yes."

"You have food?" Wallace asked skeptically.

"For now we do. As long as the generators are running the kitchen will keep making chow."

"How much longer will the generators run?"

Doctor Burke shook his head. "We have no idea. None of the maintenance personnel made it in today. I'll have them bring you down a couple plates. Sit tight."

Wallace was blown away by the doctor's kindness. He shook his hand again and said, "Thank you."

Within an hour Wallace and Chris were served chicken fried steak with mixed vegetables. They agreed it was the most delicious dinner they'd ever had. They ate in the hall while the x-ray technician took pictures of Hailey's leg with a mobile x-ray machine. After doctor Burke looked them over, he and Brenda got to work putting a cast on her leg. When they were done Brenda hurried out of the room and doctor Burke called them in.

The first thing Chris noticed when he walked in was Hailey's eyes. They were open, and not just faintly, they were wide-awake and sharp, and they followed him as he entered and sat down.

Doctor Burke washed his hands and took a seat. "Hailey here was lucky. She broke her tibia, but it was clean and she won't need surgery. Not that we could have performed surgery if she needed it." His face turned grim. "I'm sorry to tell you boys this, but we can only let you stay here till morning. We'll set you up in a room and try to get Hailey in stable condition for travel, but after that we have to let you go. As soon as we run out of power we'll have to close down. We're trying to treat and release as many people as possible before that happens."

Wallace nodded. He had a feeling their stay would be short lived. "Have you heard anything about the attack?" he queried.

"Just what the major networks are saying. I tuned in with a shortwave radio. I suppose there's some kind of video showing a missile launched from the Gulf of Mexico. Islamic extremists they say." Doctor Burke didn't sound convinced. "Do you boys live around here? Do you have somewhere to stay?"

"I live just south of Kalispell in Westfork. I'm helping Chris try to get in contact with his father, so he'll be staying with me."

"And Hailey," doctor Burke added.

For some reason Wallace hadn't thought past getting Hailey to the hospital. She was in even more of a predicament than Chris. "Yes, and Hailey too."

"Well," doctor Burke stood up, "let's go find you guys a room and you can all rest." He tapped the break lever on the hospital bed with his foot and maneuvered her toward the door. "Young man, would you push this?" he asked, gesturing to Hailey's IV stand.

"Sure," Chris said, hopping to his feet. As he neared the bed Hailey turned her head away from him. He didn't blame her.

DOCTOR BURKE didn't skimp when it came to choosing a room. Aside from the medical gas ports built into the wall by the bed, the rest of the room looked like an upscale chalet suite; complete with stained rough-hewn timber trim, a chair that folded down into a bed and an attached bathroom with a shower.

Once Hailey was situated, doctor Burke left them to rest, promising to check back as soon as he could.

Wallace was worried about Hailey. She hadn't said two words since she woke up. She just stared at the wall. The kitchen had sent down chicken fried steak that she wouldn't touch; it grew cold on the table that hovered over her bed.

Wallace took the opportunity to get a hot shower while Chris dosed on the foldout bed. Feeling refreshed and awake, he made himself comfortable in one of the chairs and pulled a small, worn, leather bound New Testament from the cargo pocket on his pants. He started reading his favorite book, Romans, and had nearly read through the whole thing when he heard a tap on the door. Doctor Burke poked his head in before sliding into the room and quietly closing the door behind him. He sat down next to Wallace and let out a deep sigh. He must have been working non-stop for the past couple of days.

"I like your choice of reading material." He nodded at Wallace's Bible.

"Oh," Wallace held it up, "thanks. It's the only book that never gets old."

Doctor Burke nodded and sat quietly for some time before breaking the silence. "I think it's going to get a lot worse before it gets better."

"I agree," Wallace said.

"I knew something like this was coming. I could see the signs. I just wish I would have taken it more seriously, prepared better."

"We all do." Wallace reassured him.

"I think it's great what you're doing for these kids," he said with sincerity.

"Just trying to do what He would do," Wallace responded, holding up the Bible again.

Doctor Burke reached into his shirt pocket and produced a prescription pad and started drawing something. "It's in times like these that we need to help each other more than ever, especially those of us who've put our faith in the good Lord." He continued to sketch out lines and scribble names next to them. "I have a ranch about twenty miles east of here," he pulled off the paper and handed it to Wallace, "this is a map. If we're going to survive this thing we can't do it alone. Come visit any time."

They shook hands again and Wallace said, "Thanks, I will."

CHAPTER 8

DUSK HAD ARRIVED when Kendrick and his men approached the Whitefish city limits. They pulled off the main road and stopped at a campground overlooking a small clear lake. The men stripped off everything that gave away the fact that they were a tactical team: vests, radios, backpacks and stowed them in the back of the truck. Rifles were also given up and hidden beneath the pile of gear. The only weapons they carried were pistols concealed under their jackets.

Kendrick reminded his men to use lethal force only as a last resort, and after consulting the map, moved into the city to find the hospital.

CHRIS STOOD in the middle of a lush, green pasture surrounded by beautiful mountains and trees. The sun was bright and high in the sky but the heat wasn't unbearable, it was warm and welcoming. He couldn't remember ever seeing such a beautiful place and although there was no sign of civilization, he felt completely at peace. He never wanted to leave.

Something moved across the pasture at the edge of the forest. A dark figure glided eerily through the shadows. The almost forgotten feeling of fear crept up the back of his neck. He couldn't move, he couldn't scream, he was frozen with terror. Chris' heart began pounding so hard he could hear it thudding in his ears and echoing off the cliff-laden mountains around him. The figure stopped. He'd given himself away. Chris knew that the figure had sensed his presence as its head slowly turned and looked straight at him.

The forest seemed to stretch and split, making a path for the dark figure to exit. The unwelcome visitor slowly stepped forward and into the pasture, allowing the sunlight to reveal his identity. It was his father, Jonathon. He approached Chris in the center of the meadow, stopping twenty feet away.

Chris searched his father's face. To his surprise, he wore an expression of fear. He was speaking, pleading with Chris about something, but as hard as he tried to communicate, Chris couldn't hear any of his words.

Jonathon beckoned to him with his hands, asking him to follow him as he started walking backward toward the trail he had emerged from.

Suddenly, the grass of the pasture started to brown and wither, and the sun felt terribly hot. Sweat rolled down Chris' forehead. Clouds rolled in from all sides and rumblings of thunder shook the ground.

Jonathon stopped and looked to the sky, then back to Chris who stood stunned and paralyzed. Jonathon began screaming Chris' name, soundlessly, and frantically waving for Chris to join him.

All at once Jonathon stood still and looked past Chris in abject horror. Chris, finally able to move, turned his head to see a shimmering star emerge from the clouds and fall into the forest behind him, followed by a searing white light. A clap of thunder rattled the teeth in his skull and an orb of fire materialized, sending out a tidal wave of flame that devoured the mountains and trees, replacing them with total darkness. Chris screamed as the fire hurled towards him. Anticipating the pain of having his flesh burned from his bones, he threw every ounce of his strength into making a run for it. He tripped and hit the ground hard.

When he got up he found himself kneeling on the hospital room floor, soaked with sweat and breathing like he'd just ran a marathon.

It took Chris a few seconds to get his bearings and realize that it had all been a nightmare. He'd slept so long that the sun had gone down. A thunderstorm had rolled in, bringing high winds, flashes of light and booms of thunder every few minutes. The lights in the room had been turned down low. Hailey was fast asleep in her bed and Wallace was slumped over awkwardly in his chair.

Chris stumbled into the bathroom and shut the door. He washed his face with cold water and held onto the edges of the sink until he stopped shaking. He had to do something to get his mind off of his disturbing dream. He sneaked from the room, careful not to wake anyone, and ventured down the hall in search of a vending machine they'd passed earlier.

It was hard not to look into the open doors of the hospital rooms as he walked. He wondered who the people occupying them were. Where would they go when the last volt of electricity had expired? What would happen to the patients who relied upon machines to deliver medicine, oxygen, life?

He shook the thoughts from his head. This wasn't any better than the nightmare he'd just had. He nodded at the big dark-haired male nurse working at the nurse's station on his left. To his right, opposite the nurse's station, was a dark room with a sign on the wall next to the open door that read 'chapel'. On the other wall of the chapel was another open door through which Chris caught site of the vending machines in the adjacent hallway. He took the shortcut and passed through the chapel. He was dying for a candy bar. He dug through his pants pockets until he found a crumpled dollar bill. After several attempts at flattening it out by rolling it over the edge of the machine, it finally accepted it and dropped a chocolate bar in the tray at the bottom.

Chris retreated to the chapel to enjoy the treat in solitude, leaving the lights off to ensure he would remain uninterrupted. He savored every nibble, fantasizing that it was a never-ending candy bar. As he enjoyed his bit of heaven a brawny man with a military style haircut strolled up to the nurse's station and started talking to the dark haired nurse. Chris wasn't particularly interested in what the man had to say, but couldn't help but over hear the conversation.

"I was wondering if you could help me." The brawny man pulled something from his pocket and put it in front of the nurse. "I'm looking for my son. We got separated and I think he may be here. He was traveling with another man and a teenage girl."

"I'm sorry, what was your name?" the nurse asked.

"Jonathon Temple. My son's name is Chris."

Chris froze mid bite. He glanced sideways at the man leaning on the counter at the nurse's station. He knew it had been a long time since he'd seen his dad, but he also hadn't forgotten what he looked like. That man was not his father. A shot of adrenaline rippled through his body. Maybe his dad had sent this man to find him, to bring him home. He decided to play it safe and hear what else he had to say before revealing his position in the dark, mere feet away.

"I'm sorry Mr. Temple, you'll have to go talk to admitting. We're not allowed to give out that information."

"Okay, I understand," the brawny man responded. "And where is admitting?"

The nurse leaned over to point him the right direction. "Follow this hallway and turn left at the –"

In one quick motion the brawny man struck the nurse in the throat with the side of his palm, sending him backwards onto the floor gasping and grabbing at his throat. His attacker wasted no time in rounding the counter and dragging the nurse through a door behind the nurse's station.

Chris dropped his candy bar. He fell on all fours and crawled behind a row of chairs toward the back of the dark room. He peaked out from his hiding place and watched for him to return. Moments later the door opened and the brawny man emerged dressed in scrubs. He stepped to the counter and rifled through papers, scanning pages, looking for what Chris could only imagine was their room.

Chris knew he had to get back and warn Wallace before the man found them. Overcome by anxiety, Chris was breathing so hard he was worried that the man might hear him. He put his own hand over his mouth and forced himself to breathe slowly through his nose.

The man tore three pages out of binder, looked around at the signs indicating room numbers and headed down a hallway that would take him away from Wallace and Hailey. As soon as he was out of sight, Chris crept to the door of the chapel and ran.

When Chris burst through the door Wallace shot straight up in his seat. He rubbed his face and gathered himself before slurring, "What's going on?"

Chris shut the door and looked for a lock. There wasn't one. He turned to Wallace in a panic. "Someone's after me!" he managed to say between gulps of air.

"What are you talking about? Who?"

"I don't know. I was eating a candy bar and this...this guy tells the nurse he's my dad, and then he killed him!" Chris was starting to cry.

"Slow down." Wallace gave Chris his seat. "Where did this happen?"

He pointed down the hallway with a trembling finger. "The nurse's station."

"Okay, stay here. I'll go check it out. Keep the door closed and I'll be back in a minute."

Chris nodded and Wallace crept into the hall, clicking the door shut behind him. It wasn't that he didn't believe Chris, but the kid had been through a lot and he could have been having a nightmare or even hallucinating.

When he reached the nurse's station there was no one there. He checked the adjoining halls for the male nurse that had been checking in on Hailey every hour. He was nowhere to be found. Wallace was starting to wonder if Chris had actually witnessed a murder. He returned to the counter and waited. Perhaps the nurse had gone into the room behind the station to get some medication. Wallace walked around the counter and gently knocked three times on the door. No response. He twisted the knob cracked the door slowly saying, "Hello," as he entered. The lights were off and he couldn't see a thing. The door stopped abruptly about halfway through its swing, something at the bottom kept it from opening fully. Wallace felt for the light switch on the wall and flipped it on. His heart jumped to his throat as his eyes adjusted to the light and he saw the body obstructing the door. The nurse lay on his back, his eyes frozen open in an expression of shock. He was dead.

Wallace turned off the light and closed the door. Chris was right, and if someone was willing to go to these lengths to find him, they were all in danger.

Wallace stood behind the counter and tried to quell the barrage of thoughts bouncing in his mind and come up with a plan when he heard footsteps approaching from the hall to his left. He swiftly moved from behind the counter and leaned on the front, acting as if he were waiting for someone. A tall muscly nurse with a military style haircut and carrying papers appeared from around the corner. Wallace didn't recall having ever seen this nurse before. His eyes were drawn to his shoes. Instead of the typical, comfortable, clog-style shoes most nurses wore, this man sported heavy soled black boots. And, he wasn't wearing a nametag.

The man gave Wallace a glance as he approached him and then went back to checking his papers.

"Excuse me, nurse?" Wallace had no idea what he was doing.

The man stopped and almost begrudgingly turned to face him. "Yes."

Wallace knew it was taking too long and it only made things worse. "Can you...tell me...where radiology is?"

The man nodded and stared at him for a few seconds. "Follow that hallway," he pointed to the one he'd just come from, "there are signs. You can't miss it."

Wallace knew where radiology was, and that wasn't the way. "Thanks," he said, then gave him a wave and started in that direction. After he rounded a bend that would take him out of sight, he briskly doubled back to spy on the nurse. The man remained near the nurse's station, probably to make sure Wallace was actually leaving, and had just entered the hallway past the chapel by the vending machines.

Wallace knew that their hall was the only one left to search. He trotted past the nurse's station, scoring an abandoned wheel chair on the way. Opening the door slowly so as not to alarm Chris, he pushed the wheelchair inside and spoke quietly and quickly. "You were right, he killed the nurse."

Chris broke down crying again.

"Hey, stop! I can't have you breaking down on me right now." He put his hand on Chris' shoulder. "I need your help. We have to get Hailey out of here and I can't do it alone."

Chris wiped his nose on his sleeve and said, "Okay."

"Get her bag of belongings and then help me get her in the chair."

Chris ran to the cabinet while Wallace went to the bedside to rouse Hailey. He squeezed her wrist and whispered, "Hailey". Her eyes opened slowly, then widened as she pulled away from him in a half-awake fit of terror.

Wallace tried to control her thrashing arms. "Hailey, stop! It's me, Wallace, the guy who brought you here. Remember?"

She stopped struggling and brought her arms in close and edged away from him, eyeing him like an ax murderer.

"Listen Hailey. There's someone coming. Someone dangerous. We need to leave now. I need to take out your IV," he stretched out his hands. "Please," he pleaded.

Still either unable or unwilling to speak, Hailey said nothing but slowly extended her arm to Wallace.

"Thank you," he said. He examined the conglomeration of tubes and tape running into her forearm and it gave him the shivers. He hated needles. The clear tape used to hold the IV in place was proving to be nearly indestructible and fused securely to her skin. He tried to be as gentle as he could, but in the interest of time he ended up firmly tugging it off her arm and pulling the IV. Hailey never made a peep.

Chris joined him at the bed and together they lifted her into the chair. They placed her belongings on her lap and adjusted the footrest to keep her leg elevated.

"I'll go first. You push Hailey and stay a few feet back. I'll signal when you can go. We need to make it to the truck. Are you ready?" Wallace asked.

"Yes," he answered earnestly.

Wallace opened the door only a sliver and pressed his face against the crack, gazing into the hall with one eye. When he was satisfied the coast was clear, he slinked into the hall and motioned Chris to follow. They inched their way toward the nurse's station where they would take the hallway running left to the emergency room parking lot. Wallace checked both ways before calling Chris forward past the nurse's station. He propelled Hailey forward, trotting behind her. The emergency room was in sight.

"Hey!" A voice from behind caused both Wallace and Chris to stop and turn around. The imposter nurse had emerged from the hallway by the chapel and spotted them. Throwing the paper he was carrying, he broke into a sprint, drawing a pistol from the small of his back as he ran.

"Go!" Wallace screamed, and pushed Chris and Hailey toward the emergency room.

"What about you?" Chris shouted.

"Just go!"

Chris heaved against the wheelchair and broke into a full run. Wallace stood his ground. If the man didn't shoot him first, he would try to at least slow him down, maybe even wrestle the gun from him.

As the man closed the distance between them he raised his pistol at Wallace. It was looking more like he *was* going to shoot him first.

Suddenly, everything went black, and the sound of machines winding down whirred in the darkness. The generators had run out of fuel.

The man cursed and his footsteps slowed. Wallace knew he was still moving forward, he could hear the rustle of his clothing and the squeak of his boots on the waxed floor. The tension in the air was thick as the darkness that surrounded them. Wallace struggled to calm his breathing. As quietly as possible, he turned and put his right palm against the wall and his left hand out in front of him and felt his way toward the exit. He was gaining speed and feeling confident that he was putting distance between himself and the gunman when something slammed into his midsection and he fell over it. At first he thought he'd been tackled but quickly determined he had ran straight into a bed that had been parked outside of one of the rooms. He groped his way around it and pulled it across the hall, blocking the way, then returned to feeling his way out. This time he kept his left hand lower.

Blue light from the thunderstorm flickered up ahead, revealing for a split second the small rectangular windows in the double doors that opened into the emergency room. He was almost there. A crash followed by more cursing echoed in the hall behind him. Wallace smiled. *Sounds like he found the bed.* When Wallace reached the doors the automatic opening mechanism was dead. He forced his way through and into the emergency room hall.

The storm outside was growing increasingly violent. Lightning struck every few seconds and radiated through the windows, unveiling Wallace's surroundings like a strobe light at a dance club. He caught site of Chris and Hailey by the sliding glass doors that led to the parking lot and rushed to them. "Why aren't you in the truck?" he whispered.

Chris pointed to the parking lot. A small truck was parked sideways directly in front of the Scout and several men were searching it, climbing through it like ants. Wallace heard the man slam into the double doors. He would be there soon.

All of the sudden Wallace remembered his shotgun that he'd stowed in the bushes just outside the door. He had to get to it quickly without alerting the men in the parking lot. He jammed his fingers into the crack in the middle of the sliding doors and forced them apart far enough fit through. He then belly crawled across the concrete and thrust his hand into the bushes. His fingers searched frantically and soon caught the hard plastic stock of the twelve gauge. He slid it into his arms and then crawled back inside. He left the door open and herded Chris and Hailey into the hall on the other side of the admitting counter. He squatted down in front of Hailey's wheelchair, grabbing Chris and pulling him down with him, and put a finger to his lips. Chris nodded that he understood. Hailey sat completely motionless, a wide-eyed zombie. Wallace took the safety off his shotgun and waited.

Sure enough, moments later the man appeared, pistol in hand, and he didn't look happy. He caught sight of the open door and immediately ran to it, assuming that was the route his quarry had taken to escape. Squeezing through the opening, he ran toward the parking lot and whistled to the men searching the Scout. This was their chance. Wallace tapped Chris and motioned to Hailey. Chris gave him a thumbs up and resumed his position pushing the wheelchair. Instead of doubling back, Wallace decided to see where the hall they were in led. Their first priority was finding a new mode of transportation.

Wallace rifled through his sling pack until he found his small LED flashlight. Turning it on would definitely give away their position, so he waited until they made it to the end of the hallway and went thru another set of double doors that read 'employees only'. Once he was sure they were out of sight, he switched it on. The light made negotiating the labyrinth of hallways much quicker and eventually they broke out into a large hallway that ended at a door with a battery operated exit sign above it.

Wallace cautiously opened the door, shotgun ready. He recognized where they were. They had come out at the rear of the hospital at the materials loading dock. The hospital maintenance shop sat to their left no more than twenty yards away, and parked in front of it, the maintenance department's abused pickup. He prayed that the keys would be in it.

Rain began to fall, sporadically at first, tapping the ground here and there, but quickly escalated into a drizzle before turning into a full-on downpour.

"Let's get to that truck," Wallace said over the noise of the rain.

"Then what? Do you have keys?" Chris was confused.

It was clear Wallace was running out of options. "Let's just get to the truck and we'll figure it out from there."

In the short time that it took them to run to the pickup, the rain soaked them all to the skin. Being drenched with frigid water combined with high winds was a recipe for hypothermia. All three were shivering uncontrollably. Luckily the doors were unlocked. Chris hopped into the cab on the passenger side while Wallace picked up Hailey and plopped her onto the seat next to him. He ran to the driver's side and climbed in. He checked the ignition. No keys. Wallace decided to risk using his flashlight, placing it between his chattering teeth so he could use both hands to check every possible hiding place for a key. He turned up nothing.

"What do we do now?" Chris asked, his jaw clenched with cold.

Wallace was finding it harder to think. He just wanted to be warm again. "Maybe the keys are in the shop." He pointed to the maintenance building. "Stay here, keep your head down and I'll be right back."

Before Chris could respond, Wallace jumped out of the truck and melted into the rainy darkness. It was awkwardly silent. Hailey's soaked hair obscured her face. She shivered hard, and her muscles twitched uncontrollably. He couldn't imagine how miserable she was dressed only in a hospital gown. In a selfless gesture he peeled off his hoody and draped it over her shoulders. She turned her head and peered at him thru steel blue eyes. He saw fear in them, and gratitude.

Flashes of yellow light moving past parked cars grabbed their attention. Someone was driving toward them through the emergency room parking lot. Chris put his arm around Hailey as they ducked below the windows. Chris offered a silent prayer, to no one in particular, asking for the vehicle to continue on without stopping.

Suddenly, the driver's door flew open startling Chris. Wallace leaned on the seat, smiled, and held up a set of keys. Chris wasn't so much interested in the keys as he was the massive amount of blood leaking from a gash on the meaty part of Wallace's palm.

"You're bleeding," he notified him.

Wallace turned his hand and gave a look of astonishment. "Wow, I didn't even feel it."

The headlights were getting closer, their beams cutting a swath through the darkness as they rounded a curve that would bring them past the maintenance department. Wallace leapt onto the seat and slammed the door just as the truck loaded with men pulled into view behind them.

They could hear the rumble of the exhaust as they idled into the loading dock area. *Keep moving. Please keep moving*, Wallace silently prayed. He heard the engine RPM's increase as the truck was put into park directly behind them. Wallace knew that if he didn't act fast this was the end of the road.

He looked at Chris and Hailey and said, "Stay down and hold on."

Still leaning over, he jammed the key into the ignition and cranked the old truck to life. He sat up in his seat, pushed in on the brake and threw the truck into reverse. The backup lights illuminated several men approaching with rifles trained on his head. He let off the brake and hopped on the accelerator. The old truck lurched, tires squealing, as it hurtled backwards. A volley of bullets meant for Wallace shattered the rear window and whizzed past his right ear, poking exit holes through the windshield. The men dove out of the way on both sides, rolling across the pavement as the pickup's rear bumper plowed into their much smaller truck and caved in the whole left side. The men's gear was thrown out of the bed along with heavy-duty plastic box that skidded across the wet pavement.

The impact threw Wallace's head into the headrest and stunned him for a moment. He shook it off and put the truck into drive and floored it, burning a U turn in the loading dock. As he drove past the wreckage he caught a glimpse of the gunman wearing scrubs pushing himself up off the ground. He couldn't help but wonder what kind of hornet's nest he'd just kicked.

CHAPTER 9

"I WANT NEW transport in five minutes!" Kendrick ordered his men as he kicked out the headlight of his demolished truck. The team sprung into action. "And get me something nice this time."

He walked over to his bag that had been tossed to the ground from the collision and pulled out the satellite phone that Jonathon Temple had given to him. He was in no mood to talk to Jonathon, but a deal was a deal. He dialed the number. Temple picked up on the first ring.

"Mr. Kendrick. Tell me you have good news. Have you located my son?"

"Yes sir, I have located him, but –"

"Is he okay?"

"He appears to be fine, but we've run into a problem."

The line was silent for several seconds then Jonathon asked, "What kind of problem?"

"It appears that your son is traveling with a group, a man and an injured girl. We tracked them to the local hospital but before I could talk to him they ran. The man he is with managed to destroy our transport and they got away."

"Let me get this straight," Jonathon was seething, "you found my son, you were within arm's reach, and an entire team of special operations soldiers weren't able to bring him in?"

Kendrick felt his blood pressure skyrocket. This was precisely why he didn't want to make the call. He'd been taking orders from weasels like Jonathon Temple most of his professional life. Men who'd never broken a sweat or seen combat calling the shots from behind oak desks in air-conditioned offices, it made him sick. He drew his combat knife to settle his nerves. "We still have time Mr. Temple. My men are working on finding a new vehicle. We should be underway soon."

"I feel so much better now that you've reassured me that we still have time." Jonathon's voice oozed sarcasm. "The next time you call you had better be able to put my son on the line. Do you think you can manage that Mr. Kendrick?"

A thousand responses popped into his head, none of which would have fostered a good business relationship. He settled on saying, "Yes sir," and hung up before he had to endure one more snide remark.

While he was on the phone, Kendrick's men were hard at work hot-wiring a giant silver luxury SUV. They tore into the parking lot and began transferring their gear into the back. Two of the men retrieved the case that housed the dirty bomb. They popped the lid, did an inspection and gave Kendrick a thumbs up.

"Load it up." He pointed to two of his men that had just finished putting packs into the SUV. "You two are with me. Let's search their room and see if we turn up anything."

It didn't take long for them to find Hailey's hospital room. Kendrick had already searched all the other patient's rooms in the other wings. He and his men used the flashlights mounted on the rails of their rifles and swept through the rooms, some still occupied by fearful and confused patients that called out for help when they saw their lights, Kendrick and his men ignored them and moved on.

At first glance there was nothing that tipped the men off that the empty room they came upon belonged to their quarry. No nametag outside the door, no personal belongings. Closer snooping revealed an IV that had been removed hastily, it still dripped into a growing wet spot on the floor, and written instructions for caring for someone with a broken leg. It wasn't until they were leaving that Kendrick noticed a small book lying on the ground next to a chair, a bible to be exact. He opened it. Something was written on the inside cover, a dedication that read:

This Bible is presented with love to my wonderful husband
Wallace MacGregor
On our 15th Anniversary
September 19th 2012

Kendrick slapped the cover shut and tucked the bible into one of his vest pockets. He had a name.

WALLACE HAD the heater cranked to 'high' as they sped away from the hospital, but the lack of a rear window nullified any warmth that it provided almost instantly. Droplets rolled off the roof of the cab and dribbled down his neck and back and his fingers were cramped painfully around the ice-cold metal steering wheel. He glanced at Chris and Hailey, still bent over, huddled together and shivering. They had to stop and get dry.

Wallace was back in familiar territory. He knew almost every road and shortcut in the valley. When they escaped the hospital he opted to avoid the highway to Kalispell, choosing instead a lesser-known back road that paralleled the main thoroughfare. He hoped their pursuers were oblivious to its existence.

They drove for several miles and turned onto a side road posted with a dead end sign. They passed a gravel pit and wound behind a small hill that would conceal them from the road. Wallace parked in a copse of pine trees and stiffly crawled out of the truck. The rain had stopped, replaced by a steady chill breeze that turned his breath to fog before carrying it away.

Cotton kills, a common saying amongst hunters and outdoorsman in Montana, kept popping in to Wallace's mind. Unlike wool and synthetic fabrics that wicked moisture away from the body, cotton retained moisture and pulled precious warmth from your skin, like a full-body parasite. Wallace knew he should have dressed differently the day he left home, and now he was kicking himself.

"Chris, I need your help."

He turned to Wallace and answered through blue trembling lips. "Okay."

"We're going to make a fire. I need you to find as much dry tinder as you can. Look under trees or anywhere else that's dry. Get dead pine needles, twigs, anything. When you think you've found enough, double it. Okay?"

"Okay," he answered, and struggled out of the truck on the driver's side.

Wallace ambled into the trees gathering larger fuel, snapping off dead low hanging limbs and forming a bundle under his arm. On his way back to the truck he happened upon a birch tree. He took the time to peel a large quantity of its flaky paper-like bark and added it to his stash.

Chris hadn't let him down; he waited for Wallace at the truck with a mound of tinder that he'd piled into the belly of his stretched t-shirt, like a kangaroo. He grabbed Chris and they cleared an area on the passenger side of the truck to build the fire. Wallace explained that hopefully the steel body of the truck would reflect heat back at them and Hailey could receive warmth by simply opening her door.

They stacked the tinder and fuel at the site. All they needed was a spark. The truck was old enough that it probably came with a cigarette lighter. Wallace leaned in to check. Of course it was gone. He paced back and forth, racking his brain for ideas when at last he remembered the steel wool pot scrubbers he'd stashed in his bag. Now all he needed was wire. Chris looked on as Wallace searched the truck inside and out, finally stopping at the rear bumper. He crawled underneath the truck bed and severed the wires that ran to the trailer wiring harness with his knife, providing several lengths about three feet long.

Wallace popped the hood of the truck and called Chris to his side. "Grab the birch bark," he instructed.

Chris willed himself to bend over to retrieve the bark, wincing against the clammy clothing that touched his skin. "Why the birch bark?"

Wallace talked as he stripped the insulation off the ends of the wires. "Birch contains oils," he wrapped an end of each wire around the positive and negative battery terminals, "it'll burn even if it's wet."

He placed the steel wool on a large piece of bark and set it on the fender of the truck. Then, taking a wire in each hand, he touched the ends to the wool. The strands of steel glowed orange and writhed into flame. Wallace carefully picked up the bark and brought it to the fire site, slowly and steadily feeding it tender and then piling on fuel until the flames grew high.

IT WAS AMAZING the effect that a simple fire could bring. Wallace and Chris thawed themselves and dried their clothes while they took shifts returning to the forest for more fuel. Hailey, who was now wearing Chris' *dry* hoody, basked in the warmth from the comfort of the truck seat.

As Wallace stretched out his hands to the heat and they regained feeling, a sting in his palm reminded him of the wound he'd sustained. On a hunch he'd broken out the window of the maintenance shop and crawled over the broken glass in his search for the truck keys. His hunch paid off, but he paid dearly. The cut was at least an inch and a half long and a quarter of an inch deep. Dirt and pine needles had worked their way into the gash, captured and cemented there as the blood dried. He cleaned it as best he could and wrapped it with an old rag he found under the seat of the truck. It was going to need stitches.

Wallace picked up his pack, laid it across his lap and dug through it until he found the small black bag. He unzipped it to make sure the remaining two bottles were still in one piece.

"What is that?" Chris was watching him from across the fire.

"Insulin." He gingerly tucked the bag into the sling pack.

"Insulin? Are you a diabetic?"

"No, not me, my wife's grandfather. These little bottles are the reason I was in Eureka."

"Can't you get that stuff around here?"

"You used to be able to. When the president came out with his executive order to ban firearms people started buying up necessities. Since pretty much no one was going to give up their guns we figured we'd better prepare for the worst. Four of us from our group split up to find insulin. I went north, my brother went south, and some friends from my church went east and west."

"How old is her grandfather?"

"Eighty-two."

"Isn't that a lot of trouble to go through for someone who's just going to..." Chris stopped himself.

The question angered Wallace and he tried his best to answer calmly. "We don't assign values to human life. Everyone has a right to live. It doesn't matter if they're old or if they haven't been born yet."

Feeling foolish for what he'd just said, Chris quickly changed the subject. "When do you think we'll make it to your house?"

"Barring anymore attempts on our life, we should be able to make it there in a half an hour. We'll leave at first light. You should try to get some sleep."

Chris agreed and tipped over where he sat. The ground was moist and uncomfortable but exhaustion won out and he dosed off.

Sleep wasn't a luxury Wallace could afford. Someone had to stand watch and keep the fire going. He couldn't stop thinking about home. He couldn't wait to see the look of relief on his wife's face, but at the same time he dreaded the lecture he would receive. *No,* he thought. *I look forward to that lecture.*

He reached for his bible in his pocket to pass the time. It wasn't there. A feeling of panic materialized in the pit of his stomach and then sadness, he'd forgotten it at the hospital.

CHAPTER 10

CHRIS WOKE to the sound of the maintenance truck's heavy door creaking open. At first he couldn't remember where he was, but the lumpy earth digging into his back quickly reminded him. The sun had begun its morning climb; its illumination causing the dark mountains to look like giant flat cardboard cut outs. He rose to find the fire that had kept him sleeping cozily was reduced to a pile of gray smoldering ashes, and Wallace already preparing to leave. Hailey was awake, but catatonic as she sat forward in the truck looking out the windshield.

"How'd you sleep?" Wallace asked, rounding the truck and stomping out what remained of the fire.

"Good. You?"

"I didn't."

Chris could tell. Wallace looked haggard and weak. His face was pale and   Chris noticed he wasn't using his right hand at all. The rag that he'd wrapped around it was saturated with rust brown blood. "Are you okay?"

"No. But I will be. Let's get out of here."

Chris wasn't going to argue with that. As he approached the passenger side Hailey moved to the middle of the bench seat. *At least she knows I exist*, Chris thought, *she just doesn't care.*

Wallace reached across with his left hand turned the key until the truck grumbled to life. They headed back down the gravel road until they met up with pavement and headed south.

Not long after they departed the sun cracked above the mountain peaks and stabbed at their weary eyes. To Chris the countryside looked like something out of a movie. There were expansive green fields as far as the eye could see, separated by miles of barbed wire fences and draped with silver-wheeled irrigation sprinklers. Every few miles a farmhouse accompanied by an obligatory red barn would pop into view, a reminder that all of the land actually belonged to someone. Chris didn't want to admit it, but he was starting to find comfort in the bigness of the land. Something about it made him feel at peace, like he was connected to something more fulfilling than a wifi hotspot.

After twenty minutes of driving the farms began to fade and it was evident that they were transitioning into the city. They came to an intersection where the traffic lights sat dead and swaying in the wind. Although traffic was nothing like it usually was, Wallace was surprised at the amount of vehicles on the road. Everyone at the intersection waited patiently for a turn, treating it just like a four way stop. Wallace turned left and followed a road that went through the outskirts of Kalispell, eventually merging into the highway that would take him home to Westfork.

Wallace was feeling the drain of exhaustion, but his spirits lifted and he felt a second wind as they hit the highway. This was the route that he travelled every day for work and he knew, without interference, he would be holding his wife in twenty minutes. His foot was getting heavier on the accelerator. Maybe it would be less than twenty minutes.

Once they were clear of the city they passed through another long stretch of farmland, but eventually the farms gave way to more and more trees as they approached the mountains. Soon, the highway was nothing more than a corridor that slashed through deep forests like an ancient subway.

Wallace's eyes were growing heavy. He tried the radio just for kicks; he wasn't surprised when he didn't find anything on. He finally resorted to squeezing his right hand every time he felt sleepy. The jolt of pain that followed seemed to do the trick. Both Chris and Hailey snoozed in their seats next to him. He was envious.

Time seemed to be playing tricks on him. It had never taken him this long to get home. Had it? After what seemed like days of driving he saw the turn ahead that led to his home in the woods. An adrenaline and anxiety cocktail shot through his arteries as he pulled onto the lane. The butterflies in his stomach thrashed about with such force he couldn't help but smile.

He turned again by a small one-lane bridge and followed the Westfork River for a quarter of a mile. Then he saw it. A quaint single level house built in the middle of a parked out acreage. Deer grazed in the front yard and mountains loomed in the background like giant sentinels. It looked as if most of the group were there. Several camper trailers were parked next to the house, and tents dotted the back yard. Months ago they had made plans with their closest friends and family. If anything were to go wrong, they would meet at their place. It's location in the foothills and close proximity to water, hunting and fishing made it the most logical place to rendezvous.

He swung onto the gravel driveway that meandered through the trees and came to a stop in front of the camper trailers. He cut the engine, waking Chris and Hailey. Before Wallace could unbuckle his seatbelt he sensed movement from the trees to his left. He turned to see someone dressed in camouflage and holding a rifle running straight toward him. It was Rob, his older brother.

"Put your hands on the dashboard!" he yelled.

Chris hand Hailey immediately complied.

"Rob!" Wallace called as he opened the door and stepped out.

Rob, slightly taller and no less burly than Wallace, lowered his rifle and pulled the camo hat off his shaved head. He stared in disbelief then ran to Wallace and engulfed him in a bear hug, lifting all two hundred pounds of him and shaking him like a doll.

"We thought you were gone," he said, dropping him to the ground.

"Not yet."

"What happened? Where have you been?"

"I ran into a little trouble in Fortine."

"Ugh." Rob made a face. "Hillbillies didn't get you did they?"

Wallace laughed. "Almost."

"Who are *they*?" Rob nodded at the truck.

"Oh," Wallace stepped out of the way. "That's Hailey and that's Chris. Guys, this is my brother Rob."

Without taking their hands off the dashboard, Chris said hello and Hailey, unsurprisingly, said nothing.

"You guys can take your hands down now," Wallace informed.

They sheepishly retracted them.

"How's Jennifer?" Wallace asked.

"It's been a rough couple of days. She's been crying a lot but she started working in the kitchen today. I think she's trying to occupy her mind." Rob stuck his finger into Wallace's chest. "She's going to kill you."

"I know. Let's get it over with."

"After you." Rob gestured to house.

Wallace walked around the truck and headed up the sidewalk to the front door. Just then, the door opened and Jennifer walked out onto the porch, unaware of Wallace's presence. She was tall for a woman, almost as tall Wallace if she wore the right shoes. The flamboyant

96

cooking apron Wallace bought her for Christmas was tied around her waist and her wild curly red hair was barely restrained in a bun on top of her head. She was drying her hands with a dishtowel and watching the deer munch on grass. Then she turned and they locked eyes. The towel fell from her grip as she cupped her hands over her mouth. Her face scrunched up and her knees started to bend. Wallace raced to her before she collapsed, wrapping his arms around her and holding her up. She sobbed and buried her face in his chest. Making fists she weakly pounded at his shoulders then wrapped her arms around his neck and squeezed him before hitting him again. It didn't bother Wallace one bit.

"I... thought... you died." She managed to say between spasms of crying.

"I'm sorry. My radio broke and the phones don't work..." Wallace decided there was time to explain later. He squeezed her tightly and said, "I'm home now."

She put her hands on his chest, pushed him back and carefully lifted his hand at the wrist. "You're hurt."

"It's just a cut, I'll be fine."

"It looks bad Wallace. Is there anything else I should know about?"

"Well, there is one thing..."

"What?" she asked, alarmed.

"I lost the bible you got me for our anniversary."

"Well, I'll just have to get you another one," she said, then she threw her arms around him again.

They hugged until Jennifer was able to stand on her own and then walked arm in arm into the house. Rob watched the whole scene as he leaned on the truck hood, shaking his head. He turned to the uncomfortable teenagers sitting inside the cab. "You guys are welcome to come inside." He stepped to the passenger door and flung it open. His eyes went immediately to the cast on Hailey's leg. "What happened to you?" She answered with a blank stare.

Chris spoke for her. "She doesn't talk much."

Rob bent over to her level and looked her in the eyes. "You want to go inside? Eat some food?"

She nodded yes. Rob slung his rifle around his back and held out his arms like one would offer to pick up a toddler. She hesitated, then moved slowly toward him. When she got to the edge of the seat, Rob scooped her as if she were a feather pillow and carried her into the house. Chris watched, unimpressed. He could do that if he wanted to. Where was this jealousy coming from? He grabbed Hailey's personal belongings and followed.

THE MACGREGOR HOUSELHOLD bustled with activity. There was hugging, crying, teasing and laughing as people surrounded Wallace. Chris watched from a safe distance until Wallace directed everyone's attention to him and Hailey. A room full of unfamiliar faces gazed at him as Wallace went down the line and introduced his compatriots. There was no way he could remember them all, but he did recall that two of the people were Wallace's parents.

Jennifer gravitated toward Hailey. She leaned in close and spoke gently to her, asking her questions to which she would answer by shaking or nodding her head. Jennifer grabbed Hailey's bag of clothes and squatting down, took Hailey's arm around her neck and helped her into her and Wallace's bedroom, closing the door behind them.

Chris joined Wallace at the kitchen table. He was showing his father and Rob his sliced palm.

Wallace's father, Frank, held his hand and examined it through his bifocals. He was a bald man with a white handlebar mustache and the forearms of a retired plumber. "This doesn't look good Wallace."

"I know."

"You should have cleaned this out immediately. Why didn't you get stitches?"

Wallace laughed. He still hadn't told the story of his last seventy-two hours. "I was a little busy. But, how's this for ironic? I cut my hand at a hospital."

Frank chuckled. "That is ironic. The cut is nice and straight but the longer you leave it open the more you risk infection. I was on a job once where a laborer cut his leg on a piece of rebar. He put off going to the doctor so long the bacteria had a chance to grow. They stitched it up and it got infected. He almost lost his leg."

"You're not making me feel any better. What do you think we should do?"

Frank cocked his head sideways as if to say it was a tough call.

Wallace shifted his eyes to Rob. "What do you think brother? You want to try it?"

"Try what?" he asked, oblivious.

"Suturing my hand."

Rob hated needles as much as Wallace. "Heck no!"

"Somebody has to do it. I think Jennifer could, but she might throw up. She's busy anyway."

"Why can't dad do it?"

Wallace didn't want to offend his father, but forty years of plumbing had left his fingers scarred and arthritic. He needed someone with a little more dexterity.

"I can't do it with these hands," Frank said.

Rob shook his head angrily. "Fine."

"Thanks buddy," Wallace said as he clapped his good hand against Rob's cheek.

He swatted it away and headed to the closet to get the first aid kit.

Wallace knew he was taking a gamble by stitching his hand after it had been exposed for so long. But, he needed to regain its use as soon as possible. He went to the kitchen sink and painfully scrubbed his hands under the faucet with hot soapy water.

Chris was watching him when it dawned on him that water was coming out of the tap. "Wait a minute. How is it that you have running water?"

"Remember kid? I'm a plumber." Wallace smiled as he dabbed his hand dry with a paper towel. "I'll give you a tour tomorrow and show you all my secrets."

Rob returned with what they called the first aid kit. To Chris it looked more like a hospital in a bag, like something you would see an EMT using at the scene of an emergency. Wallace took a seat and Frank laid out newspaper on the kitchen table and placed a clean white rag underneath Wallace's hand. Rob took out a small package that contained the needle and suture material, a tool that looked like a cross between scissors and pliers called a needle driver, and a large set of forceps. Lastly, he pulled out a medical survival book and opened to a chapter on suturing.

"This is crazy," Chris said, watching over Wallace's shoulder. "You guys have never done this have you?"

Rob looked up from reading, visibly stressed. "Do you have a better idea? Maybe you want to try."

"Rob." Wallace called his attention away from Chris.

Rob grabbed a bottle of orange liquid called Betadine solution and dumped some on a cotton ball and handed it to Wallace. He cringed as he wiped it on and around the wound. That was just the beginning, he thought; things are about to get much worse.

Next, Rob slipped on a pair of exam gloves, opened the needle package and popped open the sterile plastic bags that housed the needle driver and the forceps. Sweat was forming on both men's brows.

"I'm going to start in the middle and work my way out." Rob was talking more for his own benefit than anyone else's. "It looks like an interrupted suture is the easiest way to do this."

"Sounds good," Wallace said, trying to be optimistic.

Rob worked up his courage and said, "Okay," and moved in. He clamped the jaws of the driver onto the back half of the curved needle. With the forceps in his left hand, he gently gripped the side of the skin and opened the cut, exposing the pink flesh beneath. Starting about a quarter of an inch away he came straight down with the needle, puncturing the skin and cutting an arc toward the gash by turning his wrist.

Wallace kept his hand placed firmly on the table but the rest of his body was writhing in pain. His face turned beet red from holding his breath.

"I'm sorry buddy," Rob said consolingly.

"It's okay," Wallace exhaled.

The point appeared deep in the crease of the laceration and Rob guided it up and out. He unlatched the driver and grabbed the tip of needle and pulled it up through. The black string followed, wriggling into his hand until there was only two inches left on the standing end. He brought the needle back down into the cut and gripping the opposite side with forceps, pushed the needle through with the same arcing motion until it popped out of the skin. Wallace pounded the table with his free hand and then rested his head on the table and breathed. It was amazing how much pain one tiny piece of metal could cause.

Rob let Wallace catch his breath while he leaned over to the open book and read about how to tie a knot. He pulled the remaining suture material through, being careful not to pull the end out. Placing the needle driver parallel to and above the cut, he wrapped the string around the nose twice, grabbed the standing end and pulled it through. As the knot tightened the skin came together. Rob was careful to not make it too tight. He repeated the knot five mores times before clipping the thread with scissors.

"I just made my first instrument tie," he bragged.

"I'm so proud of you," Wallace answered, fighting back tears.

"Now we only need to do that five more times."

Wallace groaned. It was going to be a long day.

INSIDE THE bedroom, Jennifer wrapped Hailey's cast with a black garbage bag and sealed it off with duck tape just below the knee. She couldn't imagine what the girl had been through over the past couple of days, but she knew a hot shower would do a lot to lift her spirits.

While Hailey was using the shower, Jennifer went to her closet and rounded up a pair of athletic shorts and sweatshirt and set them inside the door of the bathroom. She emerged several minutes later looking cozy and refreshed.

"You look great." Jennifer was a people person who excelled at being chipper. "Do you want me to braid your hair?"

Hailey's face morphed into a slight smile and she nodded eagerly.

"Come sit." Jennifer helped her to the end of her bed and went to work separating her hair.

"Thank you." Hailey's quiet voice was an unexpected surprise.

"You're welcome, sweetie."

CHAPTER 11

THE SOUND of sizzling eggs and the smell of coffee roused Chris from his sleep. He rolled off the couch that his hosts had set up for him the night before and staggered into the kitchen. Wallace and Jennifer playfully bumped into each other as they went about making breakfast, unaware they had an audience.

Jennifer flipped eggs on an electric skillet that was plugged into a black box secured to a hand truck. Upon closer inspection Chris realized the box contained a battery and some sort of inverter. A thick cable ran from the box and Chris traced it across the floor and out the front door where it connected to a large solar panel aimed at the morning sun. Ingenious. *Too bad the rest of the house didn't run the same way*, he thought. The night before they resorted to using old oil lamps and flashlights when it got dark. Chris wondered if he would be able to charge his phone and then remembered that it wouldn't do him any good.

"Good morning." Jennifer turned to grab a knife and saw Chris admiring the solar generator. "How did you sleep?"

"I slept great, thanks."

"Would you like some eggs and coffee?"

How could anyone be this happy this early in the morning, especially in this situation? "Sure, thanks." He pulled up a chair and slumped down at the table.

Hailey emerged from the guest room propelling her self on crutches that Jennifer found in the shop behind the house. To her they were just a reminder of the knee surgery she had years ago, but to Hailey they were a symbol of freedom. She accepted them like a long anticipated Christmas present.

When Hailey entered the room Chris sat up straight and smoothed out his hair. He was struck by her beauty and felt embarrassed by how disheveled he must look. She pulled up a chair at the far end of the table.

"Hey look who's up." Wallace nudged his wife with a coffee cup.

"Good morning sweetie. Did you sleep well?" Jennifer asked.

Hailey nodded and then whispered, "Yes."

"Good. Do you want some eggs and coffee?"

"Eggs please."

"You've got it."

Chris sat in uncomfortable silence. He was afraid if he got up and left it would make things even more awkward. He stole a glance at Hailey and found her staring at him. She averted her eyes quickly and he did the same.

Wallace was watching the two and decided to take mercy on Chris. "So, Chris. Maybe later I'll give you a tour of the property and we can start making a plan on how to get you in touch with your father. How's that sound?"

"Yeah, that sounds good." Chris was thankful for Wallace's intervention.

When the eggs were done Wallace and Jennifer joined them at the table and they ate breakfast. It was a strange feeling being together, talking about the day, sharing thoughts and laughing. Chris felt like an actor in a wholesome television sitcom; he felt like part of a family.

AFTER BREAKFAST Wallace took Chris outside to show him the property while Jennifer and Hailey brainstormed on what to prepare for lunch. It was quickly becoming evident that without modern conveniences, things that didn't used to take much time required a lot more forethought and work. Before they set out Wallace gathered the vials of insulin that the group had rounded up. Rob was the only other person to find any, managing to bring back two bottles.

"I told you I'd show you my secrets today," Wallace said as Chris followed him out the back door. They walked to the north side of the house where Wallace stopped and pointed proudly to a small outbuilding with an array of solar panels mounted on the roof.

"What is it?"

"What is it?" Wallace opened the door. "It's a solar powered well pump. The sun's energy is collected by the panels, regulated by the charge controller," he pointed to a box mounted on the wall, "then stored in the batteries before it's run through the inverter."

Chris shook his head.

"This is why we have running water."

"Cool."

"You're killing me." Wallace closed the door. "Follow me."

They made their way to the south side of the house where Wallace again paused in front of a small structure that resembled a tiny slanted greenhouse. "This is why you were able to take a hot shower last night."

Chris peered through the glass front. A black tank leaned on an angle like a mummy on a display at a museum. Shiny reflective metal lined the inside of the enclosure.

"Is it a water heater?" Chris guessed.

"Exactly! It's called passive solar. I scavenged the tank out of an old electric water heater and painted it black. The sun passes through the glass, reflects off the metal and heats the water."

Chris had never been good with his hands; he never needed to be. He was actually impressed and wondered what it would be like to build something to completion that actually served a purpose. "That's pretty awesome. What about in the winter time?"

"We'll have to drain it in the winter. I haven't figured out what we'll do then. Come on, I'll show you the rest of the spread."

Wallace escorted Chris around the rest of the twenty-acre property, giving him morsels of information as they passed the chicken coop, the raised bed gardens and beehives. As they neared the back of the property another house came into view.

"Who lives there?" Chris asked.

"That's Jennifer's grandparents, Lee and Phyllis."

"Is that who the insulin is for?"

Wallace nodded. "That's right." He started toward the house. "Come meet them. They're like walking encyclopedias."

Chris jogged to catch up with him. They came out of the trees and onto their yard. The house was an old log cabin with a stone chimney built onto its side. To the right of the cabin an overgrown path penetrated into the forest.

"Where does that path go?" Chris asked.

"That's an old logging road. If you follow that you'll come out by the highway. If we have time I'll take you down there later."

Wallace knocked on the front door.

"Come in!" a man's voice called from inside.

Wallace brushed his feet on the mat and entered, Chris right behind him. Lee, a short wiry man with a full head of snow-white hair, put a book down and sat up from his recliner.

"Looks like you made it home alright Wallace," Lee said, loudly. He probably wasn't wearing his hearing aids.

"I brought you a present," Wallace said, digging in his pocket.

"What's that?"

"I said I brought you a present."

Phyllis, Jennifer's grandmother, sat on the couch and shook her head. "He probably doesn't have his hearing aids in. Lee, put your hearing aids in!"

"I don't need those things." He waved her off. "Looks like you got me some insulin." Wallace rolled the bottles into his hand. "Oh boy, that's the good stuff." He looked up at Chris. "Who's your partner?"

"This is Chris. Chris, this Lee and Phyllis."

Lee shook Chris' hand. It felt like a leathery vise. "Nice to meet you Chris."

"You too," Chris responded.

"We won't bug you anymore. We just stopped in to drop off your insulin." Wallace shouted.

"Oh, you're not bugging us. Thanks for the medicine; it should keep me going for a while. I'll throw it in the root cellar. Oh, hold on a minute." Lee tromped into the kitchen, pulled the lid off of the cookie jar and returned with fistfuls of salt-water toffee. He dropped them into Wallace and Chris' hands. "I can't eat that stuff anyway."

They thanked Lee and Phyllis, said goodbye and walked outside. Chris was already unwrapping his candy.

Wallace looked at his watch. "The tour's over, I have a meeting to go to. Do you want to see if Jennifer and Hailey need any help in the kitchen?"

Kitchen work? That seemed a little feminine for his taste, but Chris agreed without complaint in light of the fact that he would be completely lost without Wallace's help. He made his way to the house, zigzagging his way through the tents that populated the backyard, while Wallace jogged through the trees to the large shop that sat twenty yards off the east side of the house.

By the time he strolled through the large roll up door the rest of the men had already assembled. They stood in a circle in the middle of the concrete floor exchanging small talk as they waited. The men came from varying backgrounds. Wallace's dad and brother were both plumbers. Frank retired earlier that year and turned over the family business to Rob and Wallace. Next was Jeff, one of Wallace's best friends. Tall and athletic, Jeff was an Air Force vet and a barrel of laughs. Standing next to him and cradling a steaming cup of coffee was Loren, a quiet software engineer with thick glasses and the mind of a genius. And, last but not least, Wallace's nephew from his oldest brother, Micah, stood towering above the rest of the men. Micah was a Marine Corps veteran who had served two tours in Afghanistan. Although he was the youngest, there was no doubt he'd seen the most. He wasn't much of a talker, but when he did talk, it was deep. He liked to whistle. A lot.

Wallace filled everyone in on his story. Getting stranded, finding Chris, his run in with the rednecks in Fortine, and the strange squad of men seemingly bent on killing them.

"What did you say that kids last name is?" Rob asked.

"Temple. His dad is the CEO of some oil company," Wallace responded.

"Temple Petro? That kid's dad is Jonathon Temple?"

"Yeah. Why?"

"He's one of the wealthiest oil tycoons in America."

"Tycoon? What is this 1920?" Wallace jabbed.

"It's true," Loren piped up. "He ran for governor of California a few years back. He didn't win. Too many skeletons in his closet."

"Yeah, the guy is dirty alright. He's tied in with illuminati for sure." Rob shot a glance at Wallace.

"Grab your tinfoil hats boys." Wallace loved to tease Rob about being a conspiracy theorist while in reality he was just as suspicious about world events.

Rob held up his hands to quiet the laughing. "Seriously though, those men that came after you were probably sent by that kid's dad."

"Why would his dad send men into enemy territory to kill him? Maybe they were there to rescue him and I got in the way."

"You said the guy killed a nurse. Did you have any other choice *but* to run?"

"That's a good point," Wallace conceded.

"At any rate, we need to work on our security."

"Agreed. Micah, maybe we could go over that later?"

Micah nodded and resumed quietly whistling.

Wallace turned to Frank. "Dad, what are you hearing on the radio?"

Frank began dabbling in amateur radio, often called ham radio, after he retired. He set up his camper with a high frequency radio transceiver complete with solar battery backup. With the right conditions, he could talk to other operators around the world. Once they arrived at Wallace's he wasted no time in stringing up a wire antenna between two trees and making contacts. "What I'm hearing on the mainstream news is a lot different than what other hams are telling me. News reports from back east say the government called in the UN to provide humanitarian aid to the western states. I talked to one guy from Phoenix and another from Cheyenne and they haven't seen any help. Nothing. The media is also reporting that nuclear power plants in California and Washington are starting to meltdown. I haven't heard anything from California, but a buddy of mine lives not too far from the Columbia nuke plant in Washington. He says he's talked to people that used to work there and the plant is fine."

"I have something interesting," Jeff chimed in. "Before the cell towers went down I talked to my uncle who has a ranch in eastern Montana. He told me the night of the event he watched an ICBM launch from a missile silo by his ranch." He raised his eyebrows.

"The media says that missile was launched by Iranians from the Gulf of Mexico. Are you sure?" Frank asked.

"My uncle is legit. I remember him showing me the silos when I visited once. I guess they're all over the place in eastern Montana and North Dakota."

"I think it's pretty simple." Micah stopped whistling to give his two cents. "The government knew that we weren't going to give up our guns, so they EMP'd us."

"It makes sense," Loren said. "They take away our electricity and starve us out, start a war with Iran to divert attentions away from the collapse of the dollar, and by the time they're ready to bring in a global currency the people of the west will be ready and willing to trade in their guns for bread."

The group of men fell silent, as if they were grieving the loss of an old friend. Wallace broke the silence. "No. They can keep their bread. They've underestimated us."

Everyone nodded in agreement.

"What now?" Rob asked.

"We need to beef up our security. I'm aware we all know how to hunt, but we need to learn how to work as a team. We need to come to terms with the fact that we could all be here for a while. Even though we started preparing we were late to the game, and we're still lacking. We'll take stock of what we have and figure out what we need. We'll start planning after lunch."

The men disbanded, carrying with them a new sense of urgency and determination.

The ibuprofen Wallace had taken with breakfast was already starting to wear off. He unwrapped his bandaged hand as he walked to the house. Fear slammed him the chest when he saw his wound, red and inflamed. That was exactly what he didn't want to see. He quickly wrapped it before Jennifer caught sight of it. If she found out that it was infected, she would force him to take the antibiotics that they'd stored up. Knowing that they could be in austere conditions for a protracted amount of time, Wallace had resolved to only use antibiotics as a last resort.

Jennifer and Hailey were busy in the kitchen when he came in through the back. He stealthily moved into his bedroom and locked the door. Using their bathroom counter as a makeshift surgery, he laid out a pair of scissors, tweezers and a bottle of hydrogen peroxide. He pushed the tips of the scissors into the painful swollen flesh and one by one snipped the sutures and pulled them out with tweezers. He stretched out his hand to grab the bottle of peroxide and the cut split open, spilling yellow pus and blood on the counter. Wallace caught himself mid shriek and held his hand over the sink as the gash drained. He poured the peroxide over it and bit his lip. When it quit bubbling he wrapped it with a clean dressing and put on a smile before joining Jennifer in the kitchen. He hated withholding things from his wife. He felt like a liar.

CHAPTER 12

THE GIANT BOX-store that used to sell hardware and home improvement supplies now sat empty like a vandalized mausoleum, its parking lot relegated to hosting one of the largest open markets in Kalispell. People created makeshift booths out of anything they could find, old tires, pallets, some even peddling out of the back of pickup trucks, laying out merchandise on lowered tailgates.

Vendors were selling all manner of things: blankets, livestock, toothpaste and toilet paper, bibles, bullets and alcohol. The most common form of currency passed about was silver, but a lot of people were doing straight across trading. People here and there dickered over prices, never really getting too wound up since everyone was packing a gun, usually ending up with some item they believed was more valuable than the one they'd just let go.

As Kendrick crisscrossed the pavement and squeezed between shoppers, the atmosphere—even down to the smell—reminded him of a county fair. He hated it. For the past hour he'd been asking anyone that would stop and listen if they knew a man named Wallace MacGregor. He wasn't having any luck and he was nearing the outskirts of the market.

He stepped up to small camper van complete with a state-of-the-art black plastic awning held up by two broom handles and some duck tape. A middle-aged man with a goatee down to his chest reclined in a ratty old lawn chair, humming to himself and people watching. Braids of garlic hung against the side of the van behind him.

"Excuse me," Kendrick leaned into his line of sight, "I was wondering if you could help me."

"You need some garlic? Quarter ounce of silver for one braid."

"No, I don't need any garlic. I'm looking for my cousin. He lives around here, his name's Wallace MacGregor."

"Wallace? Sure I know Wallace."

"You do?" Kendrick was genuinely surprised.

"Yeah, we used to work together on jobs from time to time. That was back when people needed an electrician," the man chuckled.

"Right. Wallace is an electrician."

"No. The MacGregors are plumbers. I'm the electrician. How long's it been since you seen your cousin?"

Kendrick forced a fake laugh. "It's been a while. I just got into town from Wyoming. Wallace told me to look him up when I got here. Do you happen to know where he lives?"

The man stroked his whiskers. "No idea. But, the MacGregor's plumbing office is right on Main Street. You can't miss it. They have a big sign sticking out and all that. You sure you don't want any garlic?"

"Yes, I'm sure." Without so much as a thank you, Kendrick turned and hoofed it to his SUV.

WHEN THE DAY'S chores had been whittled down, Wallace took Chris to Frank's trailer. He explained beforehand that aside from pointing him to the nearest highway to hitchhike to California, contacting someone via amateur radio who may know his dad's whereabouts was the closest he could come to helping him. Chris

115

understood, realizing that hitchhiking was about the most stupid form of travel one could undertake considering the current circumstances.

Wallace tapped on the screen door.

"Come in!" Frank hollered.

Chris opened the door and climbed the steps. The trailer was a lot bigger inside than it looked. Wallace's mom, Esther, was knitting at the tiny dining table, her needles clicking like a slow clock. She looked up long enough to say hello and got back to it. Frank sat at a desk toward the back. He was wearing headphones and turning the dial on a large black metal box plastered with buttons and a fancy digital display. Wallace and Chris went and knelt down beside him. He stared into space, listening. After hearing nothing he pulled off his headphones and turned his attention to his guests. "What's up guys?"

"We were wondering if you could do us a favor. Chris' dad lives in California. Could you use the radio to contact someone over there that may know him? I know it's a long shot."

"It's more than a long shot, bud. Ham radio isn't like using a telephone. I can't just dial up California. It all depends on propagation and if anyone is listening. Besides that, what are the chances I'm going to contact someone that knows his father?"

Wallace was aware that the probability of reaching someone that could help in their search was slim to none. But, he didn't want Chris to think that they were unwilling to try.

"What's propagation?" Chris asked.

"In order to communicate long distances, the high frequency radio waves I transmit have to bounce off the ionosphere and then back down to earth where they're received by somebody else. How well that signal is reflected is dependent on what the sun is doing to the ionosphere at any given moment."

"Can we please try, Dad?" Wallace jerked his head toward Chris, giving Frank the most obvious hint he could.

He caught Wallace's drift. "Sure. Let's see what we can do." He pulled the headphones out of the transceiver so everyone could hear, and then fiddled with buttons and turned a big dial in the middle. The numbers on the display began to change, speeding up and slowing down according to how fast the dial was spun. Finally, Frank landed on 14.225 and picked up his microphone. "This is F7MAC calling CQ, CQ, CQ. Foxtrot seven mike alpha charlie calling CQ, CQ, CQ for anyone in California."

"That's not your call sign." Wallace said.

Frank took his finger off the microphone button and stopped transmitting. "I know. My registered call sign can be used to find out who I am, even my home address. This transmission is going just as far east as it is west. Remember?"

"Right."

Frank resumed calling, changing the frequency every so often and trying again.

Chris leaned over and whispered to Wallace, "What does CQ mean?"

"It's a left over from when messages were sent using Morse code. It just means you're sending out a call for anyone to respond."

Suddenly, a crackling voice emerged from the static. "F7MAC this is KG9."

"KG9 thanks for coming back. The name here is Frank and my QTH is the pacific northwest, over."

"Roger that Frank. The name here is Kirk and my QTH is northern California. How are things in your neck of the woods?"

"We're getting by. My loved ones are safe and we have a roof over our heads. How about you, over?"

"We're doing alright. Can't say the same for the rest of California. I talked to a buddy of mine that lives in San Diego. I guess most of the major cities have turned into war zones. When the power went out the gangs went nuts, over."

"Roger that Kirk. Say, you don't have any contacts in the San Francisco area do you?"

"Sure, I've made contacts there before. Why?"

"We're looking for man named Jonathon Temple. He was in that area when the EMP hit and we're trying to track him down."

The radio went silent for a moment before Kirk came back. "Jonathon Temple, the guy that ran for governor?" he asked.

"Yeah, that's the one," Frank answered.

"I don't want to be the bearer of bad news, but finding someone over the radio is like finding a needle in a haystack the size of California."

"We're aware it's long shot. Any information would help out."

"I could try asking around on VHF, but I can't guarantee anything."

"I really appreciate it. I'll try contacting you in two days at 18:00 Zulu time. Stay safe and 73's."

"73's to you as well Frank. KG9 clear."

Frank turned to Chris and shrugged.

"What did he mean that he would ask around on VHF?" Chris asked.

"VHF stands for 'very high frequency'. It's a band that's good for local communication. Instead of bouncing off the ionosphere it's line-of-sight. It kind of fills the gap that high frequency radio overshoots. We'll just have to wait a few days. Sorry."

Chris thanked Frank and abruptly left the trailer. Figuring he probably needed the space, Wallace stayed behind.

Chris didn't know what to feel as he stomped through the pine trees. A part of him was annoyed that the only form of communication available was so primitive. He was confused about not possessing any positive feelings toward his father, and angry with himself for wasting everyone's time. He stopped and leaned his forehead against a ponderosa. He didn't belong anywhere. Tears formed at the edges of his eyes and rolled down his face.

THE OFFICE DOOR of MacGregor Plumbing burst open and the men on the other side piled into the room with surgical precision. The office was small, only one room, and it was quickly determined that there was no one there.

Kendrick flipped open the laptop sitting on the desk. The battery had long since died. He slammed it shut. His men rifled through file cabinets filled with job estimates, bills and client lists.

Kendrick sat in the cheap, fake leather office chair and pulled himself up to the desk. He picked up and examined a small picture frame that housed a photo of a beautiful red-haired woman. He smiled. He could always use another bargaining chip. He tore open the back, removed the photo and placed it in his vest pocket.

"Got it." One of his men snatched a paper from a file folder and presented it to Kendrick. It was a Montana state plumbing license for one Wallace MacGregor, complete with home address.

"Good work."

CHRIS SAT beneath the trees for the remainder of the day, twirling pine needles between his fingertips, watching squirrels and throwing his dead phone in the air to see how close it could come to the ground before he caught it. The rest of the group must of thought he was lazy. No one sat around like him. Everyone had a job to do whether it was preparing a garden or patrolling the property. He didn't care.

As the sun slipped toward the western horizon and dusk began to fall, Hailey emerged from the house and made her way to a picnic table in the back yard. She admired the mountains, bathed in the warm orange light of the setting sun. Chris felt compelled to go over to her. He got up, dusted off his pants and sauntered over to the table.

"Is this seat taken?" His suave attempt at breaking the ice failed miserably, not even evoking the slightest response from Hailey. He sat down anyway. "Look at those mountains. You don't get a view like this in Frisco, do you?" Hailey didn't move. It was as if he was trying to contact someone in another dimension. He shook his head and started to leave.

"You left me," Hailey said. Chris froze. "Everyone left me."

"I..." Chris scrambled for a good excuse. He couldn't find one, because she was right.

She turned and faced him. "You told me I was special. That you weren't like other guys, that you would always be there for me." She shook her head with disgust. "And when I needed you the most, you left me."

Chris sat back down and ashamedly stared at the ground. He opened his mouth but no words would come out.

120

"After you got left behind, the bus ran out of gas. The bus driver went to find help. Everybody panicked," her voice began to quiver, "and they left me. Even my best friend left me."

The weight of what Hailey had been through was coming to rest on Chris' heart like a ton of bricks. It was his fault, and he knew it. He sat motionless, fighting against the growing lump in his throat. He was sick of himself, sick of having no absolutes, no convictions and no purpose. For the first time in his life he decided to face the music and take responsibility for his actions. If he didn't, he couldn't keep living with himself. He swallowed hard and met her eyes. "You're right."

An expression of shock crossed Hailey's tear-stained face. "What?"

"You're right. I left you. I chickened out. I was scared and selfish, and I should have helped you. I should have stayed. And...I'm sorry. I'm truly sorry." Tears were coming, and he could think of few things more embarrassing than crying in front of a girl, so he quickly shoved himself up from the table and returned to his sanctuary in the trees. The weight of guilt that had been crushing his spirit melted into the atmosphere as he walked.

Hailey wiped her tears on her sweatshirt sleeves and watched him as he moved away. For the first time since she had known Christopher Temple she felt like he was telling her the truth.

CHAPTER 13

WALLACE COULD SEE a change taking place in Chris. Since the night he saw him and Hailey engage in a conversation at the picnic table, the two of them started spending more and more time with each other, talking and even joking around. That same night Wallace had ventured into the trees after dark to bring Chris inside. He made it clear to him then that he and Hailey were welcome to stay as long as they needed, but they would have to start contributing. There was no room for dead weight. Chris was surprisingly accepting of the terms, and over the next two days exhibited considerable enthusiasm in learning how to chop wood, prepare the gardens for planting, and do laundry.

Hailey and Jennifer were virtually inseparable. Whenever there was cooking to be done, Hailey was right there, taking in all the secrets and tips on food preparation that Jennifer could dish out. She showed significant promise, even cooking dinner one night, with Jennifer's supervision of course. Everyone in the group agreed that it was delicious, solidifying Hailey's position as assistant chef.

It was late Sunday morning. Chris and Hailey strolled to the clothesline in the back yard, Chris hauling a laundry basket full of damp clothes for Hailey as she sped along on her crutches. The temperature in the northwest was beginning to climb as summer came into full swing and the heat of the sun's rays were invigorating. The two talked and laughed as they hung clothes. Chris teased Hailey for being too short to reach the clothesline and she retaliated by lobbing a wet t-shirt onto his face.

He couldn't remember being this happy. Actually, when he thought really hard about it, he wasn't sure he'd ever experienced happiness. Every day brought with it a sense of purpose. By splitting wood he contributed to a yet future day when the chill of winter would be rendered impotent, and working in the garden ensured food in a world where grocery stores were extinct. While they seemed strange at first, Wallace and Jennifer were turning out to be some of the most interesting people he had ever met. Their selfless love for each other and for others was unlike anything Chris had seen.

And then there was Hailey. The girl he thought he knew. When she transferred to Chris' private school at the beginning of the year he was immediately drawn to her. Sure, she was beautiful, but her parents were also the owners of a chain of organic grocery stores. She came from money, she was instantly popular, and that made Chris' pursuit of her all the more exciting. He cringed when he thought of how superficial he was. Now, he would give anything to trade all that time chasing after a higher social standing for five minutes hanging clothes with the beautiful girl in front of him.

"Chris!" Wallace called to him from the back patio and tapped his watch. "It's time."

"Okay, be there in a minute."

"What's going on?" Hailey asked.

"We're checking in with a guy on the radio. He was going to try to locate my dad."

"Oh." Hailey grew somber and picked up some more clothespins. "Good luck. I hope you find him."

Hailey's true feelings weren't easily hidden. Chris felt the same way. What if he did find his father? Would he ever see Hailey again? Would he even want to go back to the way life used to be?

"Thanks," he said. "But, it's pretty sketchy. Chances are we won't find him. Do you want help when I'm done?"

She smiled. "Sure."

"Okay." Chris walked backwards and they looked at each other, giggling like smitten kindergartners. He said, "I'll be back," then turned and met Wallace just before entering Frank's trailer.

They huddled around the desk as Frank sent out a call for Kirk. Chris was nervous, afraid of the possibility that someone had found his father. He hoped against it.

Frank tried for a solid five minutes without any luck.

"Might be bad propagation," Frank stated. "We can try again tomorrow."

"No problem—," Chris was interrupted by the crackling of the transceiver's speaker.

"F7MAC this KG9 QR zed?"

"Roger that KG9, I copy. What's the good word?"

"I'm afraid the news isn't that good." Kirk's voice was dipping in and out. Frank started pushing buttons and manipulating knobs, tuning out some of the noise. "I talked to a friend of mine that lives in the bay area. San Francisco is burning. Riots got out of hand. The place is a ghost town. He figures if somebody like Jonathon Temple were there, he probably left days ago. Sorry I couldn't help more."

Wallace put his hand on Chris' shoulder and gave it a squeeze of consolation.

"You've helped out immensely Kirk, and we thank you."

Frank finished his conversation and signed off while Wallace and Chris exited the trailer.

Wallace walked with him across the yard. "We'll keep trying. Don't worry."

"I appreciate it, but you guys don't have to keep wasting your time —"

"It's no bother. Don't worry about it." Wallace stopped abruptly, closed his eyes and wobbled. He was holding his right hand over his stomach and against his body. Something Chris hadn't seen him do since he got hurt.

"Are you okay? You don't look good at all."

"I'm...I'm fine. I'm just a bit dizzy." He shook it off, smiled unconvincingly and tried to appear energetic. "Hey, you're invited to a meeting."

"A meeting?"

"Yeah. Front lawn in two hours. Ultimate Frisbee."

Chris cracked a smile. "You got it."

AFTER A QUICK RUN THROUGH of the rules, Chris was ready to play. The men of the group skirmished and darted about on the front lawn, flinging the Frisbee back and forth until one team would score a goal by making it past the designated trees at either end of the yard.

Wallace's team was getting stomped, mostly due to the fact that the other team had the youthful energy of Chris, but partly because he felt terrible and he had to do everything left-handed.

Jennifer and Hailey sat in the shade of the deck and enjoyed the spectacle of grown men acting like boys. Mary, Rob's wife, and Linda, Jeff's new bride, sunbathed on a blanket they stretched out on the grass.

Rob intercepted a pass and everyone tore down the lawn toward the goal, everyone except Wallace. He looked confused and started walking the other way.

"What's he doing?" Jennifer asked as she stood up.

His walking slowed into a stumble and he fell to his knees and tipped forward to the ground, catching himself with his one good arm.

The men were too embroiled in the game to notice Jennifer running to Wallace.

She skidded to his side on her knees. "Are you okay?" She asked in a panic.

"I just don't feel right," he said weakly.

Jennifer put her hand on his forehead. "You've got a fever. Rob!"

Rob heard the fear and urgency in his sister-in-law's voice and spun around to see Wallace on the ground. He sprinted over and the rest of the men followed.

"What happened?"

"He's burning up, we need to get him inside."

Rob put Wallace's arm around his neck and pushed him up with his powerful legs. "Come on little brother."

Jennifer grabbed the front door and moved the dining chairs out of the way as Rob guided Wallace to the living room and dumped him on the couch.

She returned with a cold, wet rag and draped it across his forehead.

Chris stood at the end of the couch, still clutching the Frisbee. "Why does he have a fever?" His voice wavered with fear.

"I don't know," Jennifer answered. "When did you start feeling sick?" She asked Wallace.

He let out a sigh. "Promise you won't get mad?"

"What did you do?" It was too late.

He held up his bandaged hand. She gave him a stern look, then started unwrapping the gauze. Her eyes grew wide and for a moment she turned away from the nauseating site. His palm looked to be twice its normal size, bulging and fire engine red. The holes where the stitches had been removed were clearly visible on both sides of the gaping lesion and thick creamy liquid and plasma oozed down onto his wrist.

She shook her head. "Wallace."

"I'm sorry. I didn't want to break into the antibiotics. We might need them later."

She was barely containing herself. "You didn't stop to think we might need *you* later?"

"I'm sorry."

"Rob, would you help me bring the most stubborn man in the universe into the bathroom?"

He moved to the couch and helped Wallace to his feet. "You blew it this time little brother," he said under his breath.

"Thanks Rob. You're making me feel better already."

ACROSS THE ROAD from the MacGregor house and twenty yards into the woods, the forest floor shifted. A perfect six foot square of earth, complete with plants and pine needles peeled back like a blanket and two men decked out in camouflage, even painted faces, slowly and precisely rose to a crouched position. One of the men picked up a silenced sniper rifle resting on a tripod, the other a spotting scope, and together they pulled the camouflage blanket back into place.

They left their observation post and stole through the underbrush, dipping down a hill that would take them out of sight. Within minutes they met up with four other men hidden near the edge of the river.

The man handed the sniper rifle to one of his colleagues and went, by himself, to the rocky shore. He removed a satellite phone from his pocket and dialed.

"Mr. Temple. This is Kendrick. We've found your son."

ALTHOUGH SHE CAME CLOSE to vomiting several times, Jennifer managed to hold it together and scrub the infected area of Wallace's hand until only new pink flesh remained. Rob helped, steadying him at the sink and catching him when the pain became so unbearable he blacked out.

It was an ordeal for all three, and when it was finished Jennifer confined Wallace to bed and fetched antibiotics and ibuprofen from the medical supply cabinet. He was told in no uncertain terms that he wasn't to get up until he was cleared for duty.

Wallace reluctantly swallowed the pills with a swig of water and fell quickly asleep, exhausted.

They slipped out of the room quietly and shut the door. The rest of the group waited impatiently in the living room. Chris stood up as soon as they appeared.

"Is he okay? What's wrong?"

"He's doing fine for now." Jennifer spoke quietly and confidently. "He let the infection in his hand get out of control. I cleaned it and started him on antibiotics." She was silent for a moment and then her jaw started to quiver. She addressed the room through a wavering voice. "Can we please pray?"

Everyone stood and formed a circle, grabbing the hand of the person next to them. Chris was linked between the massive rough hand of Rob and the powder soft grasp of Hailey. Everyone bowed their heads and closed their eyes. Chris mimicked them.

Beginning with Jeff and moving around the circle, the group prayed aloud. They asked God for healing, protection and rest for Wallace.

Chris noticed that like Wallace, these people spoke to God like He was standing in the room with them. They prayed with authority and an expectation in their voice, like they knew what they were asking is what God wanted too.

When it was Hailey's turn Chris was ambushed by anxiety. He was next. He'd never prayed in his life, and now he had to do it out loud? It seemed rather fake to him, like he would be dishonoring Wallace by praying to his God when he didn't even believe in Him.

Hailey's prayer was short and to the point. "God, please help Wallace." She squeezed his hand, passing the prayer baton.

He couldn't do it. He stood there silently with his mouth closed, breathing so hard his nostrils might as well have been trumpets. Everyone must have opened their eyes by now to see what the hold up was. Fine. He would pray. But not out loud. It would be on his terms.

He cast his supplication into the ether of his mind. *God, if you're real – fix Wallace's hand. He's one of the nicest guy's I've met and these people need him. I need him.*

Rob's deep voice broke into prayer and pulled his attention back to the room. Chris had successfully dodged public humiliation, but he acquired something during his silent plea to the one called "God". He couldn't put his finger on it, but he knew it was there, like a song heard long ago, where the emotion of the melody remained but the tune evaded recollection.

Knock it off; you're just being sentimental. He squeezed his eyes shut even harder and focused on the sound of Rob's voice as he closed out the prayer.

After thanking everyone, Jennifer retired to the bedroom and the meeting dispersed.

Rob fell back onto the couch and rubbed his temples with his fingers. He was sitting on Chris' bed but he didn't have the courage to tell him to move. He sat down on the ottoman to wait him out.

"It's weird, seeing Wallace like that." Chris thought aloud. "For a while there I thought he was indestructible."

"He'll pull through. He's tough."

Chris chuckled. "You should have seen him beat the crud out of those creepers in Fortine."

"I can only imagine. I used to watch him fight all the time."

"Wallace?" Chris wondered if they were talking about the same guy.

"He used to fight MMA back in the day. Nothing huge, just local stuff."

"Wallace used to be a cage fighter?" He still couldn't believe it.

"Yeah. He was pretty good too."

"Why did he quit?"

Rob leaned forward. "There's something you should know about my brother. He's a nice guy, sure. But push him too far and he's got a temper like a volcano. When he was in the ring that worked to his advantage. He would tear into guys like an animal. That all changed when he became a Christian. He said he didn't like what he turned into when he fought, he didn't like hurting people."

Chris understood what he was talking about. He saw it in Wallace's eyes that day he tried to restrain himself from stomping in the man's face at the bus. Unbridled rage.

Rob slapped his knee and grunted as he left the couch. "Get some sleep kid."

CHAPTER 14

IT WAS THE early hours of the morning when Wallace's fever broke. He woke with a start. Something was wrong. It felt as if someone or something were in the room with him, a dark presence, without form, but definitely real and ominous.

He turned to make sure Jennifer was there. She was there, laying next to him, pulling long heavy breaths in a deep sleep.

He carefully swung his legs off the side of the bed and sat up.

"What's wrong?" Jennifer asked in a half conscious panic.

"Nothing, I'm fine. Just using the bathroom."

Satisfied, she instantly fell back asleep.

He popped open the door to his nightstand, grabbed his pistol and tip toed out of the room.

The dim light of a crescent moon shone through windows in the living room, causing the furniture to cast strange shadows. Chris lay flat on his back on the couch sawing logs. Wallace did a quick scan. Nothing. But the feeling was still there, getting stronger.

He raised his pistol, it felt cumbersome in his left hand, but it was better than nothing. He kept both eyes open, following the radioactive green glow of the gun's night sights as he crept into the kitchen. He stopped near the dining room table and stared at the front door and the windows on either side. Something was definitely out of place. He stood, still as a statue. The slightest movement alerted him and moved his eyes to the window on the right. The form of a man filled the frame.

His body injected itself with a shock of adrenaline and he switched off the safety. He mustered his courage and smoothly approached the window until the barrel of his pistol almost rested on the glass directly behind the head of the figure. The man was wearing a ball cap. Wallace recognized it and quickly lowered his gun and put on the safety. It was Micah, his nephew.

He unlocked the door and slipped outside. Micah stood with his AR-15, gazing into the murky forest beyond the front yard.

"What are you doing out here?" Wallace asked, whispering.

"Couldn't sleep," he answered, eyes still searching the woods.

"Me neither."

"Someone is out there."

Wallace strained to see what he was seeing. "I don't see anything."

"I can't see them, but I can feel them."

That made sense to Wallace. That's what he was feeling when he was roused from his sleep. "Who do you think it is?"

"Don't know. Every time I come around this part of the property, I feel it. I wish I had night vision goggles."

"I'll put that on your Christmas list." Wallace sat down in a wooden Adirondack chair next to Micah. "Well, we have about three hours until sunrise. I'll wait with you."

THE SOUND OF JENNIFER clearing her throat startled Wallace in his chair and he nearly dumped the pistol laying his lap onto the ground. His wife stood over him with scowl on her face, hands on her hips. He squinted in the morning light. Micah was gone but he was nice enough to drape a coat over his uncle before he left.

Wallace gave Jennifer a mischievous grin. "Oops."

"Oops is right. You said you were going to the bathroom."

"I didn't want to alarm you. I'm sorry."

She turned and disappeared into the house, returning moments later with a hot cup of coffee and his next round of antibiotics. She handed them over and slumped into the chair next to him. She could never stay mad at him for long.

"How's your hand?"

"Sore. But I feel a lot better." He downed the pill with a slug of hot coffee. 'Thanks for taking care of me," he said, putting down the coffee, taking her hand and squeezing it. She squeezed back.

They took in the early morning solitude; birds singing, two trees creaking together in the breeze, a chainsaw singing somewhere in the distance. *If this is what the end of the world is like*, Wallace thought, *then I'll take it.*

Jennifer sighed and said, "I like Hailey. She's creative and funny. She's a good kid."

"Yeah," Wallace agreed. "She's a pretty good cook too. But that might have a little bit to do with her teacher." He winked at her.

"Oh, it has everything to do with her teacher," Jennifer shot back.

"Chris is okay too. He started out as a punk, but he's getting better."

Jennifer nodded then asked, "What are we going to do with them? We can't send them to California, especially Hailey with that leg. Is there really any chance we're going to find their parents?"

"I don't think so. The best we can do is accept them into the group. Maybe someday this whole thing will get resolved, the lights will come back on and they can be reunited then."

"We should talk to the others, make sure they're okay with it, and then throw a little party for them tonight. A welcoming a party!" Jennifer was getting excited.

"Good idea. But first, coffee." Wallace held up his mug.

"Of course, coffee first."

The two were joking quietly when they both heard the sound of an engine approaching from down the road. Seeing a car pass by wasn't unusual, there were other people who lived on that road, but even normal occurrences had to be treated with caution.

A silver SUV flickered past the trees at the front of the acreage and then slowed down and turned into their driveway.

"Go get the guys."

Jennifer could tell by the tone of Wallace's voice that there was no time for questions. She darted into the house.

Wallace stood, concealing his pistol behind his left leg as he stealthily slipped it into his waste band at the small of his back.

The SUV stopped at a cautious distance and the passenger door swung open. Two hands appeared first, high above the doorframe, followed by the hulking body of a man.

Wallace recognized him immediately. It was the man that hunted them at the hospital.

"Stop right there!" Wallace yelled.

The man slowed, hands still in the air, but he didn't stop. "I'm unarmed," he hollered back.

Wallace quickly retrieved his pistol and fixed it on the man's chest. "I said stop!"

Now he was speaking a language that the man understood. He stopped.

"We don't want any trouble and we're not here to hurt anyone."

"Then what do you want?"

"We're here for the boy."

Just then, Rob and Jeff stepped out of the house and took up positions on either side of Wallace, each carrying weapons.

"Why? What do you want with him?" Wallace asked.

The man began inching toward them again. "We were sent here by his father, Jonathon Temple, to bring him home."

He moved to within twenty feet. He was probing his boundaries and Wallace knew it.

"That's far enough. You move again and I'll fire. Understand?"

The man grinned. "Sure, I understand. Can I please talk to Christopher now?"

"Well, you see, Chris might not be in the mood to talk to you since you killed a nurse and chased us with a gun."

The man laughed. "I think we've gotten off on the wrong foot. My name is Kendrick. And you are..."

Wallace wasn't going to play. "I am the man pointing a gun at your chest. I think it's time you left—"

"Wallace MacGregor. Born November 17th, 1977 in Bend, Oregon. You're the youngest of three brothers; you've been a plumber in the state of Montana for fourteen years. No children but you're married to that pretty redhead, oh what's her name," he acted like he was thinking hard, then snapped his fingers, "Jennifer, that's it."

Wallace could feel the blood rushing to his face. His breathing increased and he tightened his grip on the pistol. He didn't care that Kendrick knew his history, but his mention of Jennifer was a threat, plain and simple. *End the threat. Pull the trigger,* a voice prodded from deep inside.

Kendrick continued, "I work for very powerful people Mr. MacGregor. It's in your best interest to hand over the boy."

"He's not here. He left for California a couple of days ago."

Though Kendrick's hands were still aloft, he wagged his finger at Wallace. "Come on, we both know that's not true."

Jennifer hid just inside the open front door, listening.

"What's going on?" Chris' voice startled her. He must have been woken up by the commotion and came to the front door to investigate.

"No, go back," Jennifer frantically waved him off.

It was too late. Kendrick saw him.

"Christopher!" he called into the house.

Chris stepped onto the patio and froze with terror when he saw who was calling his name.

"Go back inside," Wallace said firmly.

Chris started to back up.

"Wait, don't you want to talk to your father?" Kendrick was a master. A snake.

Chris stopped. "H-how?" he stuttered.

"I have a satellite phone. Right here," he motioned with his eyes, "in my vest pocket. You can talk to him right now."

Chris was perplexed. In no way did he trust the murderer standing before him, but he did present an enticing offer. He'd been trying to contact his father for days without success. This is what he wanted. Right?

He glanced at Wallace who met his eyes and slowly shook his head as if to say, *don't trust him.*

Kendrick countered. "You're old enough to make your own decisions, Chris. You're your own man."

"Fine, I'll talk to him."

Kendrick locked his gloating eyes on Wallace and said, "Smart decision. I'm going to reach down with my right hand and remove the phone."

Wallace tightened his grip on the pistol and Jeff and Rob raised their rifles as Kendrick moved his hand down to his vest pocket. He tore open the Velcro closure, pulled out the phone and held it out to Chris.

"No. Toss it," Wallace said.

"Have it your way." He pitched it to Chris underhand. "Press one and hit send."

Chris stared at the phone cradled in his hand, gathering courage. He turned slowly and walked barefoot into the forest in the front yard.

"Can I put my hands down now?" Kendrick asked.

"Just keep them where I can see them," Wallace warned.

CHAPTER 15

BEFORE HE COULD think of what he was going to say, Chris dialed his dad. The longer he waited the more nervous he became. Better to just get it over with.

It purred once in his ear before his father answered. "Hello?"

Chris pulled the phone away from his head and held his thumb over the 'end' button. Hearing his voice gave him a twinge in his stomach. He could hear him calling out from the tinny earpiece. "Christopher, is that you?"

He took his thumb off the button and brought the phone back up to his ear.

"Yes, Dad. It's me."

"Thank goodness! Are you safe? Are you injured?" Jonathon's air of concern was sickening and he saw right through it. How many times had he watched his father work a prospective business partner in the exact same way?

"I'm fine, Dad."

Dead air.

"Good. That's good. I hope Mr. Kendrick didn't alarm you."

Chris snickered. "No Dad. He didn't alarm me. I watched him kill an innocent man and then he chased me with a gun. Why would he alarm me?"

"I'm sorry Christopher. I take your rescue very seriously, and that involves using people that are willing to go to any extreme to get you back. You understand don't you?"

No, he didn't. Maybe Chris from two weeks ago would understand. But, now his father's statement sounded completely asinine. Send a man willing to kill any number of people to save one persons life? Insanity.

"What can I help you with, Dad?" Chris asked, annoyed.

Jonathon cleared his throat, he was trying to stay in character but his sweet veneer was starting to wear off. "It's time to come home now. Mr. Kendrick is there to rescue you—"

"You keep saying *rescue*. Why do you keep saying that? I don't need rescued."

"Fine. Mr. Kendrick is there to bring you home. You will go with him and rendezvous with a helicopter—"

"Why?" Chris interrupted.

"Why what?"

"Why do you want me to come home?" Chris asked, emboldened by the fact that his father was hundreds of miles away.

"Because you're my son."

"Are you feeling sentimental, Dad? What are we going to do when I get home? Play catch? Toss the football around? Maybe we could go camping and have late night talks around a campfire while we cook s'mores? Let me tell you what I think will happen. You'll stuff me away in some Ivy League university. It doesn't matter that my grades weren't that great, you'll just write a check to take care of that. Then maybe you'll come visit me once a year. Visiting time is so much fun because that's where we get to have a giant argument that ends in you hitting me. Then I'll have the summer break to look forward to. You know, Dad, summer breaks at the Temple house are so much fun. I get to babysit your new wife and watch her get sloshed every day. Oh, by the way, does Madeline know my name yet?"

Jonathon erupted in a demonic growl. "Enough, Christopher!"

140

"Does she know my name?" he screamed.

"No, she doesn't know your name! What does it matter?"

Years of suppressed emotions were starting to manifest in angry tears. *No. I will not cry in front of this man,* he told himself. "So, why do you want me to come home, Dad? Do you love me?"

The line was silent for what seemed like ages before Jonathon returned. "You are very important to me Christopher. You are a Temple. We have our differences, I know, but if you can look beyond that, you'll see that you have a destiny here."

His answer only confirmed what Chris suspected. He didn't love him. His dad was a master at sidestepping the issue. To him Chris was nothing more than a vehicle, a means to perpetuate his legacy.

"Destiny?" Chris snickered. "You have it all planned out for me, don't you? You know some kids dream of growing up and being just like their dad. Not me. I don't want to be anything like you."

"That's your choice, Christopher. You don't have to be like me. But, some things in this life are beyond choice. You can't change where you came from, or what you will become. You are a Temple. It was the same for me and your grandfather before me."

"What are you talking about? What do you mean 'what I'll become'?"

Chris could hear the labored breathing of a hard decision being made on the other end of the phone. Several times Jonathon started to say something before muttering unintelligibly to himself. Finally, he drew in a deep breath and spoke. "There is a group. It was started long ago. Your great grandfather was actually one of the founding members. Our ultimate goal is to influence world events, acting behind the scenes as a sort of a guide to bring about global governance."

Chris couldn't believe what he was hearing. "Wait. You're telling me that you're a member of some secret society?"

"Not *some* secret society, Christopher—*the* secret society. Nearly everything you see happen – economic policy, executive orders, war – it's all contrived."

"Why? Why would you do that?"

"Because the masses have been deceived, Christopher. They believe that tomorrow is going to be the same as today, that the sun will rise and set, the stock market will experience an endless rally, and that oil will magically bubble from the ground for eons. They have no idea just how close the human race is to participating in its own extinction, and we Christopher, we are the ones that keep the people from stepping off the cliff. We're the unseen shepherds that herd them in the right direction. That is your destiny – to become a god."

Chris was speechless. Any semblance of his father had been overtaken by a raving lunatic with a god complex. He felt like he was living a nightmare. His father's revelations, if true, were staggering to say the least. Chris was attempting to sort through it all when something suddenly hit him.

"You were behind it, weren't you?"

"Behind what?"

"You and your weirdo friends nuked your own country!"

"Watch your tone with me!" Jonathon lashed out in his deep gravelly voice, then instantly switched back to his respectable businessman tone. "Yes, we did detonate a nuclear device, but it was carefully planned so as not to release radiation into the atmosphere. You must understand; we don't want to destroy natural resources, we want to preserve them."

"So, the purpose of the explosion was just to knock out the power grid?"

Jonathon chuckled. "Oh Christopher. You still don't understand. Why would we destroy a perfectly good power grid that would take years of labor and billions of dollars to fix? The infrastructure isn't the problem. Why destroy that? No, it's the millions of mindless sheep that occupy the west; they're the problem. They graze upon the land, devouring its precious natural resources. They're like parasites, harboring the pestilence of an obsolete ideology. All we had to do was put on a show. Give them a pretty light to stare at and then flip the switch. Their minds will make up the rest. It' the ultimate slight of hand."

Chris looked back to house. Wallace still guarded Kendrick, turning his head every so often to check on him. These people, sheep as his father called them, were the closest thing to friends that he'd ever had. Their so-called obsolete ideology fostered nothing but love and hope. Chris made his decision.

"Okay, dad. I'll come home, but not today. I want to leave tomorrow."

"Tomorrow? Why tomorrow?"

"Look, I told you I was coming home. Just give me one more day. I have some things I need to take care of."

Jonathon was silent for few seconds. "Fine. You have until noon tomorrow."

Chris started walking back to the house. "Thank you," he said.

"I have a word of caution for you Christopher. Are you listening?"

"Yes."

"What I've told you today must never be repeated, to anyone, for any reason. Do you understand?"

"Yes, Dad. I won't tell anyone."

"Good. Give the phone to Kendrick."

Chris walked to within arms length of Kendrick and carefully handed him the phone. He joined Wallace at his side.

Kendrick put the phone to his ear. "Yes sir?" His eyes studied Chris as Jonathon spoke.

"I don't trust my son Mr. Kendrick, but I'm going to give him the benefit of the doubt. Watch him closely. Like it or not he's leaving at noon tomorrow. Do whatever you have to do, just bring him back alive."

Kendrick grinned, said, "Yes sir Mr. Temple," and mashed the 'end' button on the phone. He jabbed his finger at Chris and said, "I'll see you tomorrow." He did an about face, climbed back into the SUV and drove off.

Wallace, Rob and Jeff didn't relax until the SUV was out of sight. Only then did they drop their weapons and exhale a collective sigh of relief.

"How did it go?" Wallace asked.

"I need to tell you something."

HUNDREDS OF MILES AWAY, locked away in posh office the size of a small home, the chairman of the board sat at his desk. In front of him lay a briefcase-sized black box with the lid propped open. Buttons and electronic displays adorned the inside of the lid and the bottom housed a small speaker and satellite phone resting in its molded storage place.

He had just listened to a rather disconcerting telephone conversation between one of the members of the board and his son. He shook his head and clicked his tongue against his teeth three times as if to say *tisk, tisk, tisk.*

The chairman lifted the satellite phone from the box and dialed.

THE HIDING SPOT for the SUV was only about a mile away. Kendrick turned onto the grass two-track that wound into the woods when the phone rang. *Not Jonathon Temple again. Hang in there one more day, give him back his brat and hopefully you'll never have to deal with him again.*

"Hello?" he answered gruffly.

"Mr. Kendrick?"

It wasn't Jonathon Temple. It was the chairman. Suddenly, a man that was scared of nothing became very frightened. "Uh, Mr. Chairman... I'm sorry, I thought you were someone else."

"Not to worry Mr. Kendrick, not to worry. I overheard the conversation between Mr. Temple and his son. I must tell you, I wasn't very comfortable with how much information he divulged to young Christopher."

Overheard? How? He answered the safest way he knew how. "Yes sir."

"I'm giving you a new order. We cannot risk having our plans revealed to anyone. After you retrieve the boy I want you and your team to eliminate everyone he has come in contact with. No survivors. Do you think you can handle that Mr. Kendrick?"

"Absolutely sir."

"Then I will say good day to you." The line went dead.

EVERYONE WAS SPEECHLESS. Chris stood in the middle of the shop floor surrounded by the entire group. After Wallace spread the word it took less than five minutes for everyone to assemble. Chris told them every last detail.

Rob was the first to speak. "So, let me get this straight. The whole EMP blast was nothing more than a show? You're telling me they can turn the power on whenever they want?"

"That's what he told me," Chris responded.

"Is that even possible?" Wallace asked no one in particular.

Loren piped up from a far corner. "Technically, yes." He pushed his way through the circle and crossed the room, nudging Jeff over to get at the white grease board he was blocking. He grabbed a red marker and drew a very rough outline of the United States. "The North American power grid is divided into three parts: the eastern interconnect, the Texas interconnect and the western interconnect. Each interconnect serves its respective region." He picked up another marker and drew a series of blue boxes running the length of west coast. "These are power plants, nuclear, coal, hydroelectric. And these," he drew erratic fingers emanating from each power plant that branched out across the west and ended at the Dakotas and the Midwest, " these are transmission lines. The transmission lines from the eastern interconnect don't tie in with the west or with Texas. They're all self contained. So, the east can't give power to the west or to Texas and vice versa." Loren turned to face the group, clearly in his element. "Now, it is entirely possible, through software and a satellite uplink, to simultaneously shut down the output from these power plants." He slapped the board. "If it was done right, even the workers wouldn't know it was a ruse."

146

"And you know this how?" Rob asked.

"I used to write code for a utility company before I went on my own."

Rob nodded. "Fair enough. Can it be turned back on?"

Loren ran his fingers through his hair slowly three times, thinking. "I think so. It would be a huge undertaking."

"Then we need a plan. We need to fight back and turn the power back on." Rob was getting worked up.

"We'll get to that," Wallace said. "We have a more pressing matter to discuss. They're coming back tomorrow at noon to take Chris home." He turned and looked at Chris. He'd moved out of the center of the circle when Loren took over and now stood off to the side with Hailey. "Chris, do you want to leave?"

He took a moment to look around the room. These people had accepted him and Hailey no questions asked. They fed them, taught them, saved them. They weren't strangers anymore. They were family. He ended his gaze on Hailey. She looked up at him and smiled softly. "No," he answered. "This is my home." Hailey grabbed his hand and wove her fingers into his.

"Then welcome to the family!" Jennifer cheered.

The group closed in on Chris and Hailey in a tsunami of hugs and handshakes. During the ruckus Wallace pulled Micah off to the side.

"We have some planning to do. I have a feeling Mr. Kendrick isn't going to take no for an answer."

Micah nodded, and then started to whistle.

AFTER THE WELCOMING party disbanded, Wallace and the rest of the men remained in the shop to formulate a plan. Since Chris was just as much involved as everyone else he was invited to stay.

Wallace began the meeting. "We need options and we need them fast."

"We could run," Jeff offered.

Rob shook his head. "No. We don't have enough time. We can't just pull up and leave, they would just follow us."

"He's right," Micah said. "They'll be ready if we try to run. They're much faster, better trained, and we wouldn't make it one mile."

"Then what do you propose?" Rob asked.

Micah gathered his thoughts and then approached the white board, erasing Loren's scribbles with his sleeve. "Uncle Wallace, when you were attacked at the hospital, how many men were there?"

Wallace counted in his mind. "Five. Maybe six."

"Today there were only two. Kendrick and his driver." Micah uncapped a black marker and drew an aerial view of the property including the house, the main road, the forest and the river beyond it. "I've run into people like this before – in Afghanistan. They're contractors, usually hired by the CIA, and most of them are ex special forces. My guess is they've been watching, probably for days, gathering intelligence."

"Intelligence? Like what?" Rob asked.

"Everything. Our routine, troop strength, armament, escape routes...everything."

Wallace ran his fingers over his forehead in frustration. He knew that the group as a whole was pretty lax as far as security was concerned, but when Micah started explaining the gaps in their defenses he started to get angry with himself. He hadn't taken the possibility of an outside threat seriously enough and now the safety of the entire group was at stake. "They've been watching us the whole time."

"Probably," Micah reinforced. He drew a circle in the midst of the cartoon-like trees that represented the forest between the road and the river directly across from the house. "They probably have an observation post here, manned with a sniper and a spotter. That gives them a pretty good view of the property. During the exchange tomorrow, the other two will probably be here." He drew a circle in the woods on the north and south sides of the house. "That way they can offer support up front and get anyone trying to run out the back."

Rob chuckled. "We're so screwed."

Chris felt terrible. He'd just been accepted into a family, and now he was going to get them all killed. "I'm so sorry," he said. He crossed his arms and withdrew into himself.

"You don't need to be sorry," Wallace assured him. "Finding each other wasn't an accident, and despite my brother's pessimism we're going to figure this out. Okay?"

Chris nodded once.

Wallace turned back to the group. "Ideas?"

"Here's one we haven't talked about – give the kid back to his dad," Rob offered.

Wallace gave him a shocked look of disdain. "What?"

"Think about it Wallace. The only thing we know about this kid is that his dad is behind the biggest man-made catastrophe in history. You show up with him and after a couple of days he's one of us? Why are we risking everyone's lives for him?"

"We're not having this conversation. If he leaves, I leave."

"Why can't you see—"

149

"Rob!" Frank's normally amiable character was replaced with a stern fatherly rebuke. "Let it go. The boy's not going anywhere. What good are we if we don't help those in need?"

Rob relented and held up his hands. "Fine."

Sensing a break in the awkward family dispute, Loren cleared his throat, put his hand in the air and softly said, "Routine."

Wallace pointed to him like a teacher calling on a student in class. "What was that, Loren?"

"If they've been watching us then they know our routine. For the most part it's the same everyday. They know that we're not trained soldiers and they don't expect much from us. So, if we're proactive, if we do something so outside of our routine, maybe we can gain the upper hand."

"I like it," Micah said. "We bring the fight to them."

"Wait a minute," Wallace interjected. "We're talking about human lives, we can't just go out and murder them."

Rob rolled his eyes.

"We don't have to murder them," Micah responded. "We only have to make it appear that we're in control and that messing with us would be suicide."

Wallace mulled it over, pacing in circles on the shop floor. He knew it was their only play but his mind kept analyzing, searching for any other option. There wasn't one. "Okay. Let's do it. Micah, what's the plan?"

CHAPTER 16

IT WAS LATE AFTERNOON by the time the men hammered out their plan. As soon as darkness fell one of them would create a diversion in the front yard. While Kendrick and his men were distracted, Micah, Jeff and Rob would sneak out of the rear of the house. All three would head east into the forest behind Jennifer's grandparent's house before they split up. Rob would go north, and Jeff south. Micah would also head north then loop around to the west until he found the river, following it until he arrived across from the property. It would be Rob and Jeff's job to find anyone covering the house on the north and south sides, and it would be Micah's job to get behind and locate the sniper nest. Crawling through the forest until noon the next day would be trying and uncomfortable, but the three of them were ready and willing. Even Rob.

It was decided that due to Wallace's injury, and to appear that everything was business as usual, he would accompany Chris to the driveway for the hand off. They would attempt to stall Kendrick while Rob, Jeff and Micah found their targets. Wallace made it clear that they were not to attack unless they were fired upon. The object was not to eradicate them, but to gain the upper hand and force a retreat.

"We'll use our FRS radios with earpieces to let you know when we've found our targets," Micah explained. "Starting at 0900 we'll check in every hour until noon. If things are getting out of hand and we still haven't found them, bluff. Tell them you have men in the forest and that they're surrounded. Make sure Kendrick can see your radio earpiece."

Wallace blew out a puff of air. "Never in my life did I think I would be doing something like this. I feel like I'm in a movie."

"You'll do fine. Just try to stall for as long as you can. The more nervous and agitated they get the better our chances are in finding them."

Chris stood next to Wallace as they were being briefed. He was white as a ghost.

"You okay?" Wallace asked.

"Honestly? No. What if this doesn't work? What if they kill us all?"

"We have the element of surprise. But, there's something else that we have that they don't"

"What?"

"God."

Chris admired Wallace's faith and he hoped that he was right. What if there was an omnipotent being out there somewhere – a good and just being – that *wanted* to help? Chris wanted Him on his side.

"If we're going to do this we need to get cracking," Micah said.

The men gave him their full attention. "What do you need us to do?" Wallace asked.

"Rob and Jeff both have hunting camo, but I need to make a ghillie suit."

"Tell me what you need."

SUNSET WAS FAST APPROACHING. The men spent the remainder of the evening preparing for their excursion.

Wallace found almost everything they needed for Micah's ghillie suit in the shop. Gray mechanic's coveralls served as the base for the suit. An old volleyball net was then cut and sewn down the back, legs and arms using fishing line. Chris came behind and smeared a dollop of shoe glue over each knot to ensure that it wouldn't come untied. Jeff found several burlap sacks full of duck decoys stowed behind some boxes. He dumped them out and everyone set about tearing the bags into one-inch strips. When they were finished, they colored two thirds of them with olive drab and brown spray paint. Starting at the legs and working their way up, they tied the strips onto the netting. Using a small square of netting, Micah fashioned a veil and fastened it to his ball cap. As a finishing touch, the men generously hosed the front of the coveralls with flat black, green and brown spray paint.

Micah climbed into the suit. Wallace couldn't help but laugh. "It actually turned out pretty good! You look like a Sasquatch, but it turned out pretty good."

Micah raised his arms above his head and howled like a beast, causing the rest of the men to burst out in laughter. They joked and bantered for several minutes, forgetting for that short time the dire mission that lay ahead. Wallace looked at his watch. "It's nine o'clock." The fun was over. It was time to go inside and get ready.

THE GROUP purposely left the curtains open all day. If they were being watched they wanted their voyeuristic enemy to see life carrying on as usual. Once the sun had set however, they fired up the oil lanterns and drew the curtains. It was time to make them start guessing.

Rob and Jeff donned their camo hunting clothes and smeared their faces with camouflage face paint. When they walked into the living room with AR-15's slung over their shoulders it looked like opening day of hunting season. Both men would have much rather been hunting elk; they weren't known to shoot back. Micah arrived last, a shapeless wraith in his ghillie suit. He'd painted his face so well the whites of his eyes were the only things that gave it away.

The mood of the room was solemn. Everyone realized the weight of the situation and the very real possibility that some or all of the men wouldn't be coming back. Chris couldn't put off the feeling that something bad was going to happen, and that it would be his fault. He sat down next to Hailey and clutched her hand.

"We've gathered tonight to pray for Micah, Rob and Jeff," Wallace began. "But before we do that I wanted to thank you guys, publicly. You are courageous, selfless heroes, and we love you." Everyone echoed his declaration with their own thanks and well wishes.

"Gosh. I just put this makeup on and now you're going to make it run!" Jeff joked, dabbing at the corners of his eyes.

The room erupted in laughter.

"Alright, let's pray," Wallace said. The talking stopped and everyone bowed their heads. "God, I'm going to get right to the point. We're not soldiers, well, except for Micah. We've never been in a situation like this before. But you have Lord. I think of all the battles that your people have won in the past. Gideon, Joshua, David. All of these men won battles that they shouldn't have because you were with them. We ask that the same blessing you gave to them would be given to us. Protect these men tonight as they risk their lives to protect others. May the enemy be blinded to their presence. Give us strength and courage and wisdom. We pray this in Jesus name. Amen."

When the prayer ended everyone stood and gave Micah, Rob and Jeff one last hug. Mary and Linda remained, clinging to their husbands after the rest of the group passed by.

Wallace approached delicately. "It's time," he said.

Mary nodded and her face started to twist.

"Don't cry," Rob consoled. "I'll be back tomorrow."

Unable to speak, Mary turned and buried her face in Esther's shoulder.

Linda was having trouble letting go of Jeff as well. "Don't you dare die before our first anniversary," she warned.

He tried to keep the mood light. "I'll see what I can do."

She slapped his arm, gave him a kiss and backed away.

"I'll go create a diversion," Wallace said. "Give me a couple of minutes and then you guys are good to go."

"Hold on," Loren said. He brushed passed Rob, reached out the back door and pulled in a shovel and a shoebox. "I'll create the diversion.

"What is that?"

"It's a shoebox."

"I see that. What's in it?"

He lifted the lid and smiled. "Absolutely nothing. I figured I would go bury this in the front yard. I'm sure they'll be dying to know what's inside."

Wallace laughed. "Excellent idea. But I can do it, you don't have to —"

"I want to do this Wallace. Everyone has a part. I may not be a fighter or a marksman, but I can dig a hole. Besides, you can't dig with that hand anyway."

"You're right," Wallace conceded. "Thanks." He turned his attention to the three-man squad gathered at the back door. He hugged Micah and Jeff, but Rob angled himself away and waited with his hand on the doorknob. It was obvious he was still sore over the argument they'd

155

had earlier. Wallace decided to forgo the hug and instead said, "Thank you for helping Chris."

Rob looked at Chris and then at him. "I'm not doing it for the kid. I'm doing it for them." He flicked his head in the direction of the group.

Wallace hated splitting on bad terms, but he knew his brother. *Give it a day or two; he'll cool off, if we're still alive.* "Alright everybody lights out. Loren you're up."

Frank blew out the oil lamp and Loren positioned himself at the front door.

"Go."

Loren cracked the door and slipped outside. Wallace pulled back the curtain just far enough to see him switch on a penlight and meander conspicuously around the front yard. He stopped at a ponderosa not more than twenty yards away and began digging a hole at the base. If that hadn't gotten their attention, Wallace didn't know what would. He spun to the men at the back door. "Alright guys, be safe."

They swung open the back door and disappeared into the night.

A PINPRICK OF LIGHT caught the attention of the spotter. He moved up to his night vision scope and zeroed in on its source. A man was digging a hole next to a tree.

"I've got movement." His voice caused the man sleeping next to him in the prone position to twitch and shoulder the sniper rifle in front of him out of instinct. He peered through his scope at the light source. One of the members of the group of losers they'd been watching had just laid down his shovel and picked up a box. The man looked around carefully before lifting the lid ever so slightly and peeking inside. He then gingerly set the box in the hole and began covering it with dirt.

"What do you think?" the spotter whispered. "Weapons, ammo or food?"

"Hopefully it's gold. At least we know where it is now. After we terminate these rats tomorrow we'll dig it up, split the booty."

"Right on man." They gave each other a fist bump.

CHRIS COULDN'T SLEEP. Maybe it was the couch. The first night he slept on it the cushions felt like an angelic mattress crafted from clouds. Now he was realizing just how uneven they were. An annoying lump poked at the middle of his back. He threw off his blanket and sat up. It wasn't the couch. Sure, it wasn't the most comfortable place to sleep, but if he was honest with himself, he was worried.

The moon had risen and filtered its way through the curtains at the back door. The shadows of trees were projected on to them, like a B grade horror movie on pause. Rob, Micah and Jeff were out there. No couch, no bed. They probably weren't sleeping, why should he?

Tomorrow was coming soon. Or was it already tomorrow? Normally he would check his phone for the time. He glanced at it sitting on the coffee table, dead. He snorted. *Always within arms reach and you still carry it in your pocket. What is it Chris, a blanket? A teddy bear? A drug?* He shook his head. That's exactly what it used to be, a medicinal dispensary with unlimited texts and data. A crystal ball that couldn't see the past or the future, but consumed the present. If he lived through tomorrow he would throw it in the river in celebration.

157

The muffled sound of bare feet shuffling on carpet caused Chris to turn around. Wallace came and sat on the edge of the coffee table. "Can't sleep?" he asked.

"No."

"Me neither."

"Do you think the plan will work?"

Wallace sighed. "I don't know. I keep playing scenarios over in my mind, but there's just no way to know what will happen. It's time to have faith."

"Isn't that kind of like crossing your fingers and hoping for the best?"

"Depends on what you put your faith into."

Chris knew what was coming next. He bit anyway. "What do you put your faith into?"

Wallace had him figured out. "You know the answer to that."

"Well then, when did you start believing in God?" Chris asked.

"I've believed in God for as long as I can remember, but I didn't have a relationship with him until about twenty years ago. There's a big difference between knowing someone exists and actually knowing them. I've seen the president on TV, but I've never met the guy. Don't think I'd want to anyway."

"When I was a kid my mom would talk to me about God. We had this picture bible and sometimes she would read it to me before bed. Every time I would try to envision what God looked like I would see my dad, just older. I thought, 'If God is anything like my dad, I don't want anything to do with him'."

"That's understandable. It's human nature to assign our own attributes to God. We take our experiences with other flawed people, even our parents, and assume that He's the same. But, He's not. He's ultimately good, He's unlike anyone."

Chris chewed on his bottom lip. The feeling he acquired when he prayed for Wallace had stuck with him. He tried to ignore it, to pass it off as creation of his subconscious mind. But, he knew it was more. Someone listened to that prayer. He knew that God existed, but he didn't *know* Him.

He spoke before he could stop himself. "Maybe sometime you could introduce me."

"Yeah," Wallace responded, surprised. "Whenever you want. Just let me know." It was quiet for a long time and Wallace could sense that Chris was uncomfortable with going any further. "I'm going to try to catch a few winks before morning. You should too, big day tomorrow."

"Right," Chris responded. "Good night."

Wallace returned to his room and Chris continued to gaze out the window. There was no way he was sleeping.

CHAPTER 17

BREAKFAST WAS QUIET. Chris tossed the eggs that Hailey made him around on his plate. He had zero appetite but knew that not eating them would be a colossal waste. He cut off a bite with the edge of his fork, chewed it up and forced it down.

Wallace wasn't doing much better. He hadn't touched his food. Instead, he stared at the FRS radio sitting next to his plate. It was almost nine o'clock, time for the first check in.

Frank, Loren and the rest of the group filtered in just after sunrise. Everyone was on edge and eager to hear back from the three that left the night before. They waited, impatiently, in the living room.

"Wallace, you haven't even touched your eggs." Jennifer said as she sat down next to him with her breakfast.

"I know. I'm too nervous. I'll try in a minute, after I check in with the guys." He tapped his foot nervously and checked his watch. 8:58. Close enough. "I'm going to try to contact them," he called into the living room. Everyone jumped up and huddled around the table. Wallace held up his finger, signaling them to be quiet. "This is whiskey one-six calling romeo two-six. Have you seen anything? Over."

The radio hissed and Rob's voice whispered back. "Negative."

Mary let out a sigh of relief and put her hands over her mouth.

"Roger that. Whiskey one-six calling juliet zero-three. How about you? Over."

It took longer to get a response from Jeff, but eventually he called back, "Negative."

160

Two strikes. One more try. Wallace called Micah. "Whiskey one-six calling mike one-seven. Have you seen anything? Over."

No response. Wallace tried again to no avail.

"Why isn't he responding?" Frank asked.

Wallace shook his head. "I don't know. Maybe his batteries ran out. Let's try not to assume the worst. We'll try again in an hour."

MICAH HEARD THE CALL loud and clear. But, there was no way he could respond. Although he hadn't made visual contact, he knew he was close. He chalked it up to the weird sixth sense he had about situations like these. If he spoke, even whispered, there was a chance he would give away his position.

After he and Rob headed north into the forest and parted ways, he spent the darkest hours of the night creeping slowly toward his objective, moving, stopping, listening. After he crossed the road and made his way to the river, he happened upon Kendrick's silver SUV parked in the woods and draped with pine branches. It was a good sign, but it also meant he was behind enemy lines. Instead of moving feet at a time, he started moving inches at a time. Eventually, just as the sky was turning light blue by the impending sunrise, he arrived at a mound of raised earth that gave him a good view of the landscape. To his left over a hundred yards away the road ran parallel to the river that gurgled just to his right. Beyond the road and through the trees, slivers of green siding were visible. Uncle Wallace's house. If he were going to set up an observation post, this would be the area to do it.

He sunk down into the ferns and waited.

JEFF WAS HAVING a hard time staying awake. Cracking twigs and rustling leaves kept him on edge all night and his hyper vigilance left him exhausted. Fearing that someone might sneak up behind him, he sat with his back to a huge ponderosa. Sarvisberry bushes growing at the base covered him on both sides and he had a clear view of the front of the house not more than two hundred yards away.

He'd actually fallen asleep; chin resting on his chest when Wallace called. He twitched when the radio went off and kicked up a small cloud of dust with his foot. *That's perfect Jeff, why don't you just send up a flare?* After he reported back he resorted to pinching himself to stay alert.

ROB HAD TAKEN a different approach to hiding. Instead of staying far away from the house in hopes of the enemy crossing in front of him, he chose a stand of small fir trees fairly close to the house. He lay on his belly facing the opposite direction, ready to meet any threat head-on.

"LET'S GO OVER IT again," Wallace said.

Chris cracked his knuckles and shook his hands. "Okay."

"The instant we see them coming I'll check with the guys. If they haven't found Kendrick's men I'll stall him—"

"How?"

"I don't know yet, I'll think of something. You stay right behind me. Do not, under any circumstances, move. If we can't find his men and he calls our bluff I'll tell you to run. Get to my room as fast as you can, everyone will be there, armed and ready. Rob, Jeff and Micah will high tail it back here to help out."

"What about you?" Chris asked.

He smiled. "I'll be right behind you."

Wallace checked his watch. It was 11:45. Where did the time go? It seemed like only minutes ago when he did the ten o'clock check in. Rob and Jeff still hadn't seen anything and Micah was still quiet. It was going to take a miracle to pull this off.

Jennifer entered the kitchen where Wallace and Chris were hashing out the details and hung her apron on a hook by the refrigerator. Wallace could tell by looking at her that she wasn't doing well.

"Could you give us a minute, Chris?" he asked.

"Sure," Chris said, and left to go find Hailey.

Jennifer stood with her hands on her hips looking at the floor. Tears were already starting to drip from the tip of her nose. Wallace put his arms around her waist and pulled her in close. She hung her arms around his neck rested her head on his shoulder.

"I can't do this," she cried.

"Do what?"

"Risk losing you again."

A lump started to grow in his throat. "There's always a risk. I could get hit by car on the way to the store."

"You know what I mean," Jennifer retorted.

"No matter what, in the end, we'll be together. You know that right?"

"Yes, I know." Jennifer pulled her head back and locked eyes with him. "You promise me that you'll be careful. Don't do anything stupid!"

"I promise."

Jennifer laid her head back down and broke into a sob. "I love you."

Wallace squeezed her tight. "I love you more."

CHRIS FOUND HAILEY at her favorite spot, the picnic table in the back yard. She loved to look up at the mountains. He sat down and admired them with her.

"I don't feel like a kid anymore," she said without breaking her gaze.

"Yeah, it's funny how fast you grow up when you have to," he agreed.

"It seems like yesterday that I moved to California, started a new school, a new life. I never thought I would end up here...with you. I find myself feeling guilty, because in a weird way, I'm glad things turned out the way they did. I mean, don't get me wrong, I miss my parents and my sister—"

"Hailey." Chris needed to say something and he didn't have much time. She turned and looked at him.

"Yes."

He grabbed her hand and wrapped both of his around it. "I'm an idiot..."

"I know," she said. They both laughed.

"But, seriously. When I first met you I liked you. But, it was childish, immature infatuation. You said you don't feel like a kid anymore. Neither do I. I've grown and I know things now that I didn't before." He looked at the sky, searching for the words. "I guess what I'm trying to say is...I love you."

Hailey's eyes grew wide. "I—"

"Don't say anything! I just wanted you to know before this all goes down today. I love you...I love you."

He squeezed her hand, turned and left. She sat speechless as he walked away.

CHRIS JOINED WALLACE at the front door. It was 11:55.

"Showtime everybody!" Wallace declared.

Frank and Loren, armed with shotguns, ushered Mary, Linda, Hailey and Esther to the bedroom. Jennifer sneaked Wallace one last kiss before slipping in last. Frank gave Wallace a thumbs up and closed the door.

"Are you ready for this?" Wallace asked.

Chris' stomach was full of rabid butterflies, his heart pounded and he was forcing himself to take deep breaths. "I think so."

Wallace put his hands on his shoulders. "You'll do fine."

They walked out onto the front patio. They were outside for barely a moment before they heard the sound of a car coming their way. *There's no way he's that punctual,* Wallace hoped. He was proved painfully wrong when the familiar silver SUV appeared.

He keyed his radio. "Guys, this is it. Please tell me you have something." He released the button.

Rob replied, "Negative."

"Negative," Jeff answered.

Still no Micah. He keyed the radio once more as Kendrick turned down the driveway. "Stand by guys, this could get hairy. God bless."

The SUV stopped and the driver cut the engine. Kendrick swung open the door and walked straight toward them, stopping at roughly the same spot he'd stood last time. Wallace noticed that he never moved directly between him and the road. *You're giving your sniper a clear shot aren't you? Smart.*

"Beautiful morning isn't it?" Kendrick was gloating.

"It'll be even more beautiful once you're gone." Wallace replied.

"Then let's get it over with. Hand over the boy and we'll leave. Never to be seen again."

Wallace had to stall, to try to get him riled up. "About that. How do I know you're not just going to kill us all once we hand him over?"

Kendrick grinned. "I'll tell you what. I'll give you my word. How about that?"

"Not good enough. I want a guarantee."

"A guarantee? What is this? You're not buying a car. All you need to do is hand over the kid and we're out of here."

Wallace was grasping at straws, but it seemed to be working. Kendrick was getting agitated. "I want it in writing, from the kid's father."

Kendrick cursed and turned around, shaking his head. He turned back, his confident evil grin replaced with bulging eyes. "You must be dumber than you look you inbred redneck! How am I supposed to get a written guarantee out here?" He lifted his hands in the air.

"That's your problem. That's what I want, so you figure it out." Wallace knew he'd pushed too far. Kendrick drew his pistol in the blink of an eye and held it on him.

"Here's my guarantee. If you don't hand over the boy in three seconds I'm going to drop you like a dirty shirt. Three...two..."

"Wait!" Chris held up his hands behind Wallace. "I'll talk to my dad. He can guarantee their safety, just don't kill anyone."

"No! No more talking. Walk to me and let us take you home."

"I'm not going with you unless you let me talk to my father. I'm sure you're getting paid a pretty penny for bringing me in. How much do you get if I show up in a body bag?"

Wallace was surprised. Chris knew how to negotiate.

Kendrick thought hard for a moment. He knew they were going kill them all once they had Chris, something he was looking forward to, but if the bullets started flying now there was a chance the boy could get wounded or killed. And, if that were the case, his payday would be bleak. He holstered his pistol and tore open a pocket on his vest, producing the satellite phone. "You have exactly three minutes," he said, stretching it out toward them.

"Ah, ah. Toss it. Remember?" Wallace reminded him.

Kendrick's face pinched into a look of sheer hate. He tossed it underhand to Wallace, who then passed it over his shoulder to Chris. He pressed one, then send. One ring. Two rings. *Come on dad, pick up of the phone.* Three rings. The line clicked. "Kendrick, do you have him?"

"It's me dad."

"Christopher? It's so good to hear your voice. I trust everything went well. You should be home within—"

"I haven't left yet."

"What? Why not?"

"I want you to do something for me."

"We don't have time to play games Christopher, go with Mr. Kendrick now!"

Chris spoke quietly but sternly, hoping that Kendrick couldn't overhear the conversation. "I'm not playing games. Listen to me. For

167

once in your life I want you to do something for me, no strings attached, no hidden agenda that benefits you. I want you to make me a promise."

"What kind of promise?"

"If I come home, I want you to promise to leave these people alone..."

Wallace turned his head and looked at him over his shoulder. This wasn't part of the plan. "Chris, what are you doing?"

Chris continued, "You have to promise me that you won't harm them in any way. Can you do that?"

JENNIFER WAS A BUNDLE of nerves. She paced the floor of the bedroom. *What is taking them so long?* "I'm going out there," she said, reaching for the door handle. Frank grabbed her arm.

"No. Jennifer, it's not safe. I can't let you."

"They're taking too long. Something isn't right."

"We need to wait for them to come and get us. Please, stick to the plan."

She looked her father-in-law square in the face. "Dad, I *need* to be with Wallace. I *need* to be."

"There's a reason you're in here. I'm supposed to protect you."

"If something happens to him I'm as good as dead. You have to let me go."

Frank could tell by the look in her eye that he could plead with her until he was blue in the face; she wasn't changing her mind. He let go of her arm. "Okay," he said. "But stay out of sight."

Jennifer quickly and quietly exited the room. She kept her back to the wall and slid around the perimeter of the living room. She peeked around the corner. She could see Wallace through the window standing on the patio as Chris talked on the phone behind him. Kendrick was out of sight, standing to Wallace's left, so she tiptoed across the kitchen and through the dining room landing against the wall next to the window. Her husband was mere feet away, separated by a pane of glass. She could hear everything.

"WHAT YOU'RE ASKING of me is impossible Christopher." Jonathon replied.

"No, you're just incapable of making a promise to your son."

"It's not like that."

"Then what is it like?" Chris was done trying to be quiet.

"I can't guarantee their safety because the plan is already in motion and I don't have the power to stop it."

"What plan? What are you talking about?"

Jonathon tried to evade the question. "There's no time—"

"I'm hanging up," Chris threatened.

"No! Christopher!"

"Tell me, what plan?"

"Kendrick and his men aren't there just to get you. They're part of a mission to detonate a radioactive dirty bomb. They're going to set it off there, Christopher. If you don't leave you could suffer side effects, you could die."

Chris' jaw dropped. "A dirty bomb? Why? Why would you do something like that? You...you have to call it off. You can stop them..."

"No. I can't. The chairman of board has already made the decision. You must leave now, Christopher. Please."

Chris looked at Kendrick and then at Wallace. It was apparent that they'd both heard him say 'dirty bomb'. For the first time since he'd known him he could see fear written on Wallace's face. Kendrick gave him a devious sideways glance while he nonchalantly inspected his fingernails. Chris could hear his father begging for him to answer. Suddenly, the course of action seemed perfectly clear. Chris knew what he had to do, and somehow, knowing there was only one choice brought peace. *Whatever happens, happens. God, it's up to you.* He pushed the phone to his cheek and spoke over Jonathon. "I don't know who you are, but you're not my father. I'm not leaving...goodbye." He hung up the phone.

One side of Wallace's face lifted in a half smile. Chris smiled back. They were committed now. It was time to bluff. Hopefully the three sentinels waiting in the forest were ready for whatever was coming next.

"Doesn't sound like things went too well with daddy. You two can work things out when you get home. Let's go." Kendrick held his out his hand and gestured to the SUV.

"He's not going anywhere." Wallace's voice cracked. *Steady Wallace, you need to sell this.* He straightened and added some tone. "Get back in your car and leave while I'm being generous."

Kendrick chuckled. "Who do you think you are? What makes you think you're in any position to make demands?"

"We have you surrounded. Last night my people slipped into the forest and located your men...all of them." He turned his head and tapped his radio earpiece. "We've been in contact all morning. So, I'll tell you who I think I am. I'm the guy with the upper hand, the backwoods moron that outsmarted you. I'm the guy with his finger on the big red button, and when I say 'boo' we put you and your friends down for a dirt nap. That's who I am."

170

Kendrick stood expressionless, then burst out laughing so hard he had to bend over and put his hands on his knees. He composed himself and wiped his eyes with the backs of his hands. "Your people in the woods huh?" Kendrick turned his head and tapped on his ear just as Wallace had done. He had a flesh colored earpiece, far smaller and more advanced, hidden in his ear as well. "You mean the two men you have in the woods over here?" He pointed north and south with each hand. A jolt of adrenaline rocketed up the back of Wallace's throat. "We've been listening to you all morning." He clapped his hands together. "So, you want to gamble? Let's gamble. I'll see your two men and raise you six highly trained combat veterans. One of which," he held his left index finger in the air next to his head, "is a spectacular sniper. What say you? Will you hand over the boy?"

"No."

Kendrick shook his head. "Okay. Drop her," he said, whipping his finger to the ground.

The air by Wallace's right arm seemed to warp for a split second and the window behind him popped and split into thousands of fragments, followed immediately by the report of a high-powered rifle. Wallace and Chris both ducked and threw their hands up to protect their faces.

Moaning came from within the house. Jennifer.

"Wallace? Wallace? Oh no, Wallace I've been shot!" she screamed.

Nothing else mattered. The bullet could have traveled through him before hitting her; he didn't care. Wallace ripped open the front door. His wife lay on her back clutching her right abdomen, dark blood trickled from between her fingers and pooled on the tile floor. He dropped to his knees at her side. "No, no no. You're going to be fine. Somebody help!" he bellowed. "Dad! Help!" In shock, he looked around frantically. This couldn't be real. His mind fractured. So much so, that he watched as Kendrick threw a shoulder under Chris and lifted him off the ground. He carried him to the waiting SUV and threw him into the back seat.

CHAPTER 18

THE AROMA OF BURNT gunpowder wafted through the air. The close proximity of the gunshot startled Micah. But, years of training and experience won out. He didn't flinch. He was hoping he would find the sniper before he got a shot off. The best he could do now was keep him from taking another one.

He scanned the forest floor in front of him. They were either wearing ghillie suits like him, or they'd constructed a mat and pulled it over themselves. All he needed was one out of place bush; one odd movement and he would have them.

Seconds passed. Time was running out. Micah decided that he would stand up, give away his position and hopefully force the enemy to reveal themselves. He put his palms on the ground to push himself up when he heard it; the bolt of a rifle sliding back, then forward, chambering a round. It came from his left. He froze and searched for anything out of the ordinary. Something moved forty feet away. Two lumps that he mistook for moss covered tree stumps shifted down ever so slightly. *Gotcha.*

THE SNIPER TOOK AIM at the man leaning over his wife. He couldn't believe that first shot hadn't killed her. How did he miss? The reflection in the window must have thrown him off. *I won't make the same mistake twice.* He put the crosshairs on the man's spine, center mass.

Kendrick's voice called through his radio earpiece. "We have the boy! Wipe them out. When you're done we'll circle back and pick you up. I repeat, weapons free!"

The sniper and spotter turned and looked at each with pleased smiles. The spotter whispered, "This is gonna be fu—"

Before he could finish a bullet exited his forehead and sprayed flecks of blood on the sniper's face. He fumbled for his sidearm, throwing off the mat and rolling onto his back. He fought the Velcro strap that held it in the holster, but it was too late. A wraith stood over him and fired two rounds through his skull.

FRANK AND LOREN burst out of the room when they heard Wallace call out. They found him kneeling in a pool of blood and rocking back and forth over Jennifer. Frank rushed to his side. Jennifer was still conscious; she was in overwhelming pain, but conscious.

Wallace looked up at his father with fury in his eyes. "They shot her. She didn't do anything and they shot her!"

Frank shared his anger but knew they were sitting ducks. "We need to move her to the living room—"

No sooner had the words escaped Frank's lips and the other window shattered. Bullets tore through the doorframe by Wallace's head and poked holes in the drywall inside the foyer.

Frank and Loren jumped back and took aim. At what? They had no idea where the fire was coming from. Wallace stuck his hands under Jennifer and with a growl, picked her up and ran to the living room, laying her gently on the couch. Frank and Loren retreated to the kitchen where they took cover behind the refrigerator. The firing subsided.

"Oh, it hurts!" Jennifer moaned.

Wallace grabbed her hand, still covering the wound. "Let me see."

She lifted her trembling fingers and Wallace peeled up the hem of her blouse. The bullet had grazed the right side of her pelvis, shredding a path through her flesh the length of his index finger.

"Is it bad?" she asked.

"Loren!" Wallace yelled.

"Yeah?"

"I need the first aid kit."

"Right."

Loren appeared with the kit and Wallace rifled through it until he found a battle dressing. He tore open the plastic wrapper, placed the trauma pad over the wound then passed the elastic bandage under her back and wound it snugly around her torso.

Beads of sweat were forming on Jennifer's brow and she slid her left leg up and down, searching for an outlet for the pain. "Where's Chris," she asked.

Wallace looked up as he fastened the bandage. "They took him."

"No. You have to get him, Wallace."

"I'm not leaving you."

Jennifer reached down grabbed Wallace's bloodstained hands, taking them in hers. She rallied her strength and spoke to him calmly. "You know it's the right thing to do. Go get him."

Wallace looked down at his wife's delicate fingers, painted brown with dried blood. What did she do to deserve this? A woman who'd devoted her whole life to being a force for good, a safe haven?

A fire of rage began to claw its way up the small of his back, spreading out across his shoulders and forcing up the hair on the nape of his neck. He clenched his teeth and his muscles tightened. *He did this to her. He took Chris. He's going to pay.*

JEFF didn't know exactly where the shots were coming from, but they weren't anywhere near him. It sounded like world war three had broken out. He knew his objective was to find anyone sneaking through the woods from the south, but it was obvious things had not gone according to plan. The fear that the enemy might have been forcing their way into the house convinced him to abandon his post.

He slowly stood, gathered his rifle and started in that direction. He'd made it three steps when he heard an ear-shattering crack. Before he knew what was happening he was propelled forward, face down on the ground, stunned. A searing pain immobilized his left shoulder—so cold it felt hot. He'd been shot.

He let go of his rifle and brought his right arm up under his chest, trying to roll over. Footsteps approached from behind. He stopped. *This is the part where you go to heaven, Jeff. Sorry Linda.* The tip of a boot slipped under his useless shoulder and heaved him over on to his back. A commando stood over him—painted face, full camouflage—something out of an action movie.

"My name's Jeff. What's yours?" He'd never taken things too serious. Why start now?

The man didn't answer. Instead he let his rifle hang over his chest and yanked his combat knife from its sheath.

"You call that a knife..." Jeff taunted.

The man grinned and bent over. As he did, something ripped through the side of the pack on his back. Confused, he stood back up and looked over his shoulder. A gunshot echoed through the forest. Jeff could tell by the look on the man's face that he knew it was too late to run. With a hollow smack, a hole appeared in the man's chest six inches below his chin, followed by the echo of another shot. He tipped over backward, his legs twitching for a moment before they slowed then stopped.

Micah's voice hissed over the radio, "You're welcome."

IF ROB WERE PRONE to bouts of emotion, he would have sprinted for the house at the first shot. Fortunately, he wasn't prone to bouts of emotion, allowing him to remain motionless and hidden as he listened to something prowl through the underbrush in front of him. He waited, patiently still, as a soldier emerged and opened fire on the front of the house.

He would take him down. But, it would be at the right time—when the shot presented itself. This was hunting.

The man trotted forward past Rob's left side and stopped against a tree twenty yards away, steadying his rifle barrel against the trunk.

Patience Rob. Wait for him to go past.

The man waited for several minutes, checked his scope, then moved past the tree and toward the house. Rob turned on his belly, keeping him in sight. The man rested against another tree, his back turned to him. Rob lowered his head and peered through his scope, placing the illuminated red dot on the back of his quarry's head. *This is hunting Rob. Take a deep breath, let it out slowly, squeeze the trigger— don't pull.*

The rifle jumped in his hand and nudged his shoulder. The man dropped. Rob rested his head on the ground, sick to his stomach. This wasn't hunting; it was killing. His brother's voice, first calling to him from the house then on the radio, caused him to look up. Wallace needed him.

Rob yelled into his radio. "Does anyone have visual on more targets? How many are there?"

"I think that's all of them," Micah came back. "Head for the house, I'll cover you."

"Where's Jeff?"

A weak voice came over the radio. "I'm hit."

"Rob, get to the house. I'll get Jeff after you're clear. Go!"

He scrambled to his feet, broke cover and ran, full out, for the house. He met Wallace as he was rushing out onto the front patio. He was carrying his shotgun and a set of keys.

"Is everyone okay?" he asked Wallace.

"Get in the truck, you're driving," he said without stopping.

"What happened, is everyone alright?"

Wallace stopped abruptly, turned and exploded. "They shot Jennifer!" he snarled, eyes wide and crazed. "And they took Chris."

"Is she…"

"She's hurt, but she'll live. Are you going to drive or what?"

Rob snatched the keys from his brother's hand. They jumped inside the hospital maintenance truck and Rob cranked it to life.

"They're going to hit the highway before we can catch up." Rob informed.

"Use the logging road. We'll try to cut them off."

178

He threw the truck into reverse and gunned the accelerator, twisting the wheel at the last moment so the front of the truck whipped around. He dropped it into drive and flew down the gravel driveway, hung a left, and sped toward Jennifer's grandparent's house. He aimed for the small tunnel in the trees at the end of their yard. The truck floated over the manicured lawn and plunged into the forest. Overgrown limbs reached into the road and slapped the windshield and raked the fenders. Though they'd been down that road over a dozen times, it had always been walking or riding an ATV, not drifting around corners at forty miles per hour.

By the time Wallace spotted the ditch carved across the road by the spring run-off, it was too late to notify Rob. They charged into it at full speed. Wallace bounced off his seat, bumped his head on the roof and slammed back down with a spine-jamming thud. The rusty pipe rack fixed to the truck bed jounced twice, slid, and tumbled off onto the road. The men looked at each other and then reached over and buckled their seatbelts in unison.

IT WAS OVER. Chris had just seen one of the sweetest women he'd ever met mercilessly gunned down in front of him. The man responsible then picked him up like a toddler and forced him into his car, restraining his hands behind his back with zip ties. Now they hurtled toward the highway, toward Chris' father, toward his 'destiny'.

At least his captors didn't make it out unscathed. Chris could hear Kendrick calling his men over the radio—they weren't responding. Eventually he gave up and turned to the last man he had left, the driver.

"They're gone. Stop just before the highway. We'll deploy the bomb there."

"Yes sir," the driver responded.

Chris looked over his shoulder into the cargo area. A green plastic case was locked to the deck with two ratcheting tie-downs. It didn't look sinister, but then again neither did his dad. *I guess it really is true; it's what's on the inside that counts.* On the inside. Chris thought of the quiet voice in his heart that had been persistently whispering to him. He couldn't understand what it was saying; maybe it wasn't even using words. But, he could feel what it meant. He likened it to when his mother would call for him to come inside when it was getting too dark out to play. Beckoning. Love.

Chris closed his eyes. *God, I've been a terrible person and I don't even deserve to talk to you. I know you exist. I tried to tell myself otherwise, but I'm through trying to deny it. God, I need your help. Please stop these people. Don't let them hurt anyone else...*

"Praying isn't going to do you any good." Chris opened his eyes to see Kendrick turned in his seat, staring at him. "You're going back to your father and I'm..."

Kendrick's words trailed off. A flash out of the corner of Chris' eye diverted his attention. He turned, and for a split second he saw the red pickup surge from the forest on his right, then it smashed into the side of the SUV.

Metal. Glass. Mayhem. The truck's front end melted into the SUV's passenger side front fender, whipping it around until the sides of the two vehicles were touching. Together they barreled into the ditch and bounced into the forest where they plowed to a halt.

No one in the SUV had been wearing a seatbelt. If it weren't for the airbags deploying, Chris probably would have flown out the back door window. He lay face down on the floor in the back seat, coughing from the powder off the airbags. His arms were still restrained behind his back and he couldn't find a maneuver that would help him sit up.

Wallace blacked out. The force of the impact and weight of his own body against the seatbelt were too much for him. He woke to the sweet smell of antifreeze and melting rubber. To his left, Rob lay slumped over the steering wheel.

"Hey," he punched his shoulder, "wake up." He didn't move. "Rob, wake up!" He hit him harder.

Rob moaned and slowly lifted his head. "Stop punching me," he said, lids half open. He looked out the window at the steaming wreckage of the SUV. "Whoa. I was aiming for the rear quarter panel."

"I think you were off...just a bit."

The brothers were still gathering their wits when they heard a door on the SUV creak open. The driver stumbled out and caught his balance on the hood. He looked at them, turned, and then took off running into the woods, weaving and tripping like a drunkard.

"He's getting away!" Wallace yelled. He yanked on the door handle. It didn't budge.

"I got him," Rob said, unbuckling his seatbelt and crawling out his window. He set out after him, looking no less intoxicated as he ran.

Wallace could hear coughing. The passenger seat was empty. Either Kendrick was thrown from the vehicle or he was slumped over. Either way, Wallace hoped he was dead. He undid his seatbelt and crawled out his window. His side was killing him. Some ribs were definitely broken. He hobbled around to the driver's side, peeking in the open door at the empty front seats. A pistol lay on the passenger side floor. No Kendrick. Compared to the rest of the car, the rear door appeared brand new. He lifted the handle and swung it open. Chris looked up at him from the floor and started laughing, then crying.

"Come on, let's get you out of there," Wallace said, grabbing him by the shoulders and pulling him straight out. Chris got his legs under him and fell forward onto Wallace, burying his face in his shoulder.

"I thought I'd never see you again," he sobbed.

Wallace put his burly arms around Chris and squeezed. "Nobody steals a member of my family."

Chris sniffed and brought his head up. He was about to say something when he looked past Wallace. His eyes grew huge with shock. The sole of a boot struck Wallace between the shoulder blades, sending him and Chris flying onto the backseat of the SUV. All of the oxygen was kicked out of Wallace's lungs. He struggled to drag air in through his nostrils. A giant hand grabbed the back of his collar and pulled so hard he thought his head was going to come off. He travelled through the air backward and flopped flat on his back. Kendrick stood over him.

"I blame myself for this," he said, wiping blood from a cut above his eyebrow. "I really should have killed you the first time I saw you. It would have saved me a lot of trouble, and men."

Wallace rolled to his belly and tried crawling away on his elbows, wheezing. Kendrick walked next to him slowly, observing him like a hunter waiting for a wounded animal to die. He made it to a small lodgepole pine, pulled himself up on the trunk and flipped around, leaning his back against it. Kendrick's giant fist collided with the side of his head and he tipped over like a falling tree. The world phased in and out. *No Wallace. Do not go out. Hang on...*

Searing pain exploded in his side at his broken ribs and his body moved. Kendrick landed a massive kick into his midsection. He exhaled a groan of agony and curled into a ball. Through his fading vision,

Wallace saw Kendrick pull his leg back for another kick. *This is it.*
Suddenly, Chris, hands still tied behind his back, jumped in front of him,
screaming and kicking at his attacker like a wild animal. Wallace took
the few seconds of distraction to force himself onto all fours, gain his
balance and stand up.

Kendrick seemed more annoyed with Chris than anything,
absorbing blows like he was indestructible. He brought back his hand
and caught Chris across the face. He hit the ground. Out cold. Kendrick
snickered, spit, and then turned back to Wallace. A surprised look
crossed his face as Wallace brought up his fists, clenched his jaw and
tipped his head down. He let out a half-hearted chuckle and lunged with
a right hook. Wallace dodged and jabbed his jaw with his left,
immediately following with a right straight into his teeth. Kendrick
wobbled and brought his hand to his mouth. His bottom lip was split
and dripping blood. Wallace hit a lot harder than the kid.

He blew blood and saliva out of his mouth and charged Wallace,
throwing his shoulder into him and tackling him to the ground. He
landed on top and Wallace wrapped his legs around his torso. Kendrick
let loose with a barrage of punches to his face. All he could do was cover
and wait for Kendrick to get tired. His punches started to slow and
Wallace peeked through his forearms. Kendrick changed his angle of
attack and instead of coming straight down at his face, swung up at his
chin. His knuckles connected under his jaw and slammed his teeth
together. All motor skills were lost and he dropped his arms.

Wallace was somewhere between consciousness and death. He
was aware that he was being pummeled—his head whipped from left to
right, absorbing punches. But, there was no pain. He wasn't afraid that
he was going to die. What bothered him most was that he'd failed.

Jennifer would cry again at the loss of her husband, this time for real, and Chris would be delivered to his insane father.

The punches stopped. Wallace's eyes were closed but he felt Kendrick's breath as he leaned in close to his face and spoke with sick pleasure in his voice. "I want you to know something. After you're dead, I'm going back to your house. I'm going to finish the job. I'm going to kill everyone you love, and I'm going to take my time."

He wrapped his massive fingers around Wallace's throat and began to squeeze like a boa constrictor. The thought of Kendrick torturing his family, laying his hands on his wife, drifted through his mind and ricocheted through his synapses. Something deep within him began to stir. Absolute rage. He opened his eyes, aware that he only had seconds before the supply of blood was completely cut off from his brain. He grabbed Kendrick's arm with both hands and flattened it against his chest. The shocked look on Kendrick's face pleased him and he smiled at him with crazed eyes. Wallace threw his legs around his torso again, this time using his hips and oblique muscles to maneuver. When he had Kendrick where he wanted him he shifted quickly and brought his left leg over the side of his head. He lifted his hips, simultaneously pushing down with his legs. He had Kendrick in a textbook arm bar. His muscular arm was stretched to its limits over Wallace's chest. Kendrick let go of his throat and tried to use all of his strength to prevent his arm from breaking. At this point in a professional fight Kendrick would have tapped out and Wallace would have been declared the victor. Wallace wasn't interested in a win by submission. He roared like lunatic as every muscle strand in his body pulled back. Kendrick screamed as his arm snapped backward at the elbow with a sick pop.

Wallace released Kendrick from the hold and both men scrambled to their feet. Wallace resumed his fighting stance as Kendrick stared at his dangling arm in horror. Taking advantage of his stunned opponent, Wallace jumped forward and planted his foot into his chest. Kendrick stumbled backward against the SUV and Wallace leapt forward and slapped his cupped hands against the sides of his head, shattering Kendrick's eardrums. He howled in pain and shook his head, trying to clear the disorientation.

Wallace went berserk. His fists flew—body, face, body again—splitting flesh and collapsing bone structure until Kendrick's knees buckled and he collapsed on the ground. He rolled over and slid his left hand over to his right hip and drew his knife. Wallace immediately stepped on his forearm, grabbed the knife from his hand and tossed it over his shoulder.

Both looked like they'd been through hell and back. Wallace staggered to a nearby tree and wrapped his arm around it to keep from falling over.

Kendrick dropped his head to the ground, exhausted. "Finish it. Come on, kill me," he said.

Wallace looked at him for a moment and then answered, "No. I'm not a killer."

Kendrick laughed. "You could've fooled me." He fumbled to his feet. "You'll have to excuse me...I have mission to complete." He limped to the SUV and lifted the hatchback. The dirty bomb still sat secured in the cargo area. Kendrick loosened the release levers on the straps and threw them off.

"Stop!" Wallace commanded, out of breath.

He flipped the latches on the container and lifted the lid, revealing a silver cylinder connected to a digital keypad by strands of multicolored wires. "There are no options. Succeed or die." He brought his finger up to arm the bomb. Wallace moved in from behind and slid his arm under his chin putting him in a rear naked choke. Kendrick pulled against him, gripping the edge of the case and pulling himself forward. Wallace flexed his arms and straightened his back.

"Don't make me do this," he whispered.

Kendrick didn't give up. He stretched his fingers out to the keypad, face red and eyes bulging, until his arm slowly fell. His body went limp and Wallace walked back with him, gently laying him on the ground. He released his hold and pushed his fingers into the valley next to Kendrick's throat. No pulse. He was dead.

Wallace felt he'd lost something deep inside of himself. Innocence. He was furious at the dead man lying at his feet. Kendrick had robbed him of his ideals and forced him to compromise his beliefs. Though he was gone, the damage he'd caused would stay with him forever.

As he looked at the lifeless body in front of him, he saw the ruffled pages of a small book protruding from Kendrick's vest pocket. He shoved his fingers around it and pulled it free. It was his bible. He clutched it to his chest and began to cry.

Chris groaned and moved. Wallace wiped his eyes and crawled to him.

"Are you alright?" he asked, helping him sit up.

"I think so. Can you cut me loose?"

Wallace found Kendrick's knife lying by the driver's side door and cut Chris' restraints. He rubbed his wrists and then his jaw.

"Is he dead?" Chris asked.

Wallace looked away and nodded.

"Thank you...for coming after me."

"You're welcome."

Wallace helped Chris to his feet. A branch snapped in the distance and they both turned to see Rob stomping towards them through the woods.

"Did you find him?" Wallace hollered.

Rob shook his head and waited to speak until he'd made it to them. "I chased him for a long time, but he got away. He's probably to the highway by now." He looked at Kendrick. "What happened here?"

"He was going to detonate the bomb," Wallace said, voice shaking. "He wouldn't stop. I had to..." His voice choked off.

Rob put his hand on his shoulder. "It's okay. You did what you had to do."

Somehow that didn't make Wallace feel any better.

The three looked at the bomb sitting dormant in the back of the SUV. They all agreed that it was too dangerous to just leave there while they hiked back to the house, so they heaved it out of the back and hid it in the woods.

Rob and Chris each took one of Wallace's arms around their neck and they started down the logging road. Soon, they would be home.

CHAPTER 19

JONATHON TEMPLE LOOSENED his tie and poured himself another drink. He wasn't celebrating, but he did intend to get very, very drunk. He'd just managed to lose his son and put the board's plans in serious jeopardy. At Zimmerman's last update it was believed that all six members of the retrieval team were dead or MIA and the dirty bomb was neither armed nor detonated. Phase two was a complete failure and he'd divulged privileged information to a boy who'd chosen a group of rebels over his own father. He had no hand in Kendrick's failure to deploy the bomb, but someone would be blamed. He had a pretty good idea who that would be.

"To you Jonathon." He lifted his glass to himself and threw back the remaining alcohol.

There was a knock at the door.

"Come in."

Zimmerman poked his head in. "Excuse me sir, do you have a moment?"

"Of course, Zimmerman. Come in. Would you like a drink?" He filled his glass.

"No thank you, Sir."

"Sit down, relax," Jonathon said, gesturing to the chair in front of his desk.

"Sir, the board is moving into phase three. The chairman has requested your presence at his office in New York."

Jonathon swallowed a gulp of whiskey and slammed the glass down. Brown liquid flew into the air and splashed all over the desktop. It was a lot closer than he thought. He belched and shook his head. "You know what, Zimmerman? I'm really not in the mood to see the chairman. Tell him I'm busy," he slurred.

Zimmerman looked uncomfortable. "I'm sorry, sir, you really don't have a choice."

At that moment two men in suits stepped through the door and stood on either side of Zimmerman.

"Ah, I see," Jonathon said. He straightened his tie, downed his whiskey, and was escorted out of the room.

FOR A MOMENT WALLACE didn't know where he was. When he was waking he envisioned himself in his own bed, but when he opened his eyes and saw the log walls and rough-hewn timber floors he suddenly remembered that he was in Dr. Burke's guest room. Jennifer lay next to him sleeping.

It was their third and final day at the doctor's house. Rob, Chris and Wallace returned after their showdown with Kendrick to find Jeff barely conscious and dying, and Jennifer's hip beyond the scope of any of their medical knowledge. Wallace remembered the map that Dr. Burke had drawn him, and Frank rushed them to Whitefish.

The doctor, being a good and gracious man, took them in and did his best to patch them up with what he had. Wallace had four broken ribs, a broken nose and a dislocated cheekbone. Jennifer's gunshot wound, though painful, was far from lethal. Jeff nearly died the first day, but pulled through and began making leaps and bounds in his recovery.

Unfortunately, Dr. Burke lacked the proper equipment to do more than patch him up. The bullet had lacerated tendons and destroyed his shoulder. He wouldn't regain the use of his left arm. The news brought sadness to the other members of the group, but, true to his style, Jeff made light of the situation and took some of the edge off. It didn't hurt that Linda had branded him a national hero and volunteered to be his personal nurse.

Dr. Burke insisted that he feed them breakfast before they left. His wife, Anne, a jovial silver haired angel, cooked them all steak and eggs and they ate their fill. They thanked them repeatedly as they left, and the Burke's told them they were welcome at the ranch anytime.

When they returned home they found that the rest of the group had been busy as well. Rob, Micah and Loren salvaged all the equipment they could from bodies of Kendrick and his men, finding several automatic rifles, a sniper rifle, spotting scope, night vision goggles, radios and a large cache of ammunition. They loaded the bodies of the men onto Rob's flatbed truck and hauled them to the mountains, burying them under piles of rocks.

There was one final task to attend to. That evening, Wallace, Rob and Chris returned to the site of the crash. They siphoned the remaining gas from the maintenance truck and the SUV into plastic containers. They then retrieved the dirty bomb from its hiding place and loaded it onto Rob's truck. They needed a place to stow the bomb, somewhere no one would find it, but also somewhere that would contain the blast if it suddenly decided to go off on its own. Rob knew just the place.

The three piled into the truck and crossed the highway onto a gravel road. They followed the road for miles, winding higher and higher up the mountain until at last they broke into a large leveled off area. It was a dead end.

The rocky face of the mountain projected toward the sky in front of them, and as Rob pulled closer Chris saw a black hole carved into its side – an abandoned mine.

They backed the truck to the entrance, unloaded the bomb and carried it deep inside.

THE NEXT DAY the group attempted to return to normalcy. Chris helped Wallace repair the front door jam and cover the broken windows with lumber they scrounged from around the property.

That evening the group gathered to discuss the future. They'd been entrusted with delicate information that possessed the potential to derail the plans of the enemy. Now they had to decide how best to use that information.

There was also a very real possibility that Kendrick and his men wouldn't be the last of the unwelcome visitors. One of Kendrick's men had managed to escape. He knew their exact location – their strengths and weaknesses. Drastic changes would have to take place if they were going to have any chance of survival.

THE SUN WAS SETTING. Chris stood on the front porch and watched as the daylight gave its encore and exited stage-east.

The familiar squeak of Hailey's crutches came up behind him. She stopped next to him and laid her head against his shoulder.

"Do you want to go for a walk?" he asked.

"Sure."

They walked through the trees in the front yard, inhaling the cool night air, and sauntered across the road and entered the forest on the other side. A deer trail wound through trees and they followed it until they emerged at the bank of the Westfork river. No more beautiful place existed on earth. The sky glowed orange and pink where the sun had gone down and it reflected in the river like a shimmering fire that was cool enough to touch. The night was serene and the gently flowing river provided an amazing soundtrack. Chris reached into his pocket and pulled out his phone—the embodiment of who he used to be. Without so much as an inkling of regret, he drew his arm back and cast it out into the river.

Hailey let her crutches fall on the rocks. She took Chris' face in her hands and gave him a single kiss. He wrapped his arms around her and they embraced until the fire in the sky went out.

The light had gone and the forest was dark and ominous, but Chris smiled all the way home. He stomped the mud from his shoes onto the patio and opened the door for Hailey. As she passed by something caught his eye. Was something glowing in the grass?

"You coming?" Hailey asked from inside.

"Yeah, I just have to check something. I'll be there in second." He pulled the door closed and stepped over to investigate. It was the satellite phone, and it was still on. Chris bent over and picked it up. The screen said "two missed calls".

He pushed the power button and turned it off. After checking to make sure no one had seen him, he shoved it in his back pocket and went inside.

EPILOGUE

A Blackhawk helicopter flew so low that it nearly grazed the treetops. It had no markings and its flat green paint made it invisible against the mountains.

Inside the cargo area, four children not more than ten years old sat huddled together on a hard steel bench seat. They were horrified. Across from them a monster in a yellow rubber suit peered at them through the soulless dark eyepieces of a black respirator.

They'd first met him two weeks earlier, after being rescued by a U.S. border patrol agent while sneaking across the border from Mexico. The people who took them in were nice. They spoke their language, gave them food, clothes and a place to sleep. But, when the monster in the yellow suit arrived he was different. Rough. He stuck a needle in their arms—the same one—and then took them outside and loaded them into a van. They were driven for hours until they arrived at an airport where they were forced into a helicopter by the monster.

The helicopter slowed, lifting its nose for a moment. It rotated a quarter turn and touched down in an open field.

The yellow monster opened the door and pointed for them to disembark. They were paralyzed with fear. It reached across and backhanded a little boy across the thigh and pointed again. With a scream the boy got up and jumped from the chopper. The others quickly followed. It slid the door shut behind them.

The Blackhawk's engines whined and it lifted and fluttered off. The children turned around. A city skyline sprawled out in the distance.

One of the buildings seemed very strange to them, a tall skinny tower with a saucer sitting on top. They looked at each other, and with nowhere else to go, started walking toward the city.

The Adventure Continues

Book two by Seth Evanoff

THE CHAOS REBELLION

Available Spring 2015

www.ingramcontent.com/pod-product-compliance
Lightning Source LLC
Chambersburg PA
CBHW061200170626
46809CB00003B/1189